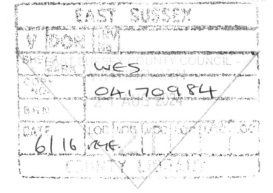

Shadow of the Noose

When he learns that the young man who saved his life is to hang for murder, Ben McCabe knows that the only way he can rescue Tommy Kane from the hangman's noose and prove his innocence is to arrange a jail-break. Then he must go in search of the real killer.

Time is against him as he comes into conflict with the powerful Dexter family, whose youngest son Kane is convicted of killing. McCabe runs into a veil of secrecy before coming face to face with the man who left him for dead.

Shadow of the Noose

Peter Wilson

A Black Horse Western

ROBERT HALE · LONDON

ISBN 978-0-7090-9163-9

Robert Hale Limited
Clerkenwell House
Clerkenwell Green
London EC1R 0HT

www.halebooks.com

Typeset by
Derek Doyle & Associates, Shaw Heath
Printed and bound in Great Britain by
CPI Antony Rowe, Chippenham and Eastbourne

ONE

The stranger hitched his horse to the rail outside the small barber's shop. His attention was drawn to the small group – mostly children – at the corner of the street and from out of sight came the noise of heavy hammering.

He rubbed his chin, ran his hand through his long, untidy hair and decided that his curiosity could wait. He needed a shave and a haircut more than he needed to know what was happening around the corner of a small out of the way Arizona town. But his guess was that he had come to the right place.

He had barely settled into the chair before the barber, a spindly old-timer who had clearly been in the job for more years than he could remember, broke into his thoughts.

'You in town for the hanging, mister?'

'That what all the banging's about down the street?'

'Sure is. We ain't needed gallows in Rico since we strung up a couple of killers back before the war. We could have used a tree outside of town but this kinda makes it more legal.'

The barber paused to examine his handiwork.

'Who's going to hang?' the stranger asked, trying to stem the man's enthusiasm for what had been made to sound like a Saturday night at a dogfight.

'Kid called Kane – a bit of a no-hoper around town.'

'Who did he kill?' He already knew the answer.

The old man paused, his cut-throat razor hovering dangerously close to his customer's eyebrow.

'Dave Dexter. Put a coupla bullets in his back.'

The man in the chair stayed silent, well aware that the barber would be keen to elaborate. He didn't have long to wait.

The old man sighed. 'And all over a woman. I suppose it was gonna happen some time. Just a pity for young Kane he picked on the Dexter boy.'

'How so?'

The barber paused in mid stroke and chuckled.

'You sure are a stranger in these parts, mister, if you ain't heard of the Dexters.'

'Hey! Steady with that razor.'

The barber put down his cut-throat and started to towel the man's face.

'Tommy Kane had been walking out with Ellie Jacobs – pretty young thing, daughter of old Doc Jacobs. Anyway they seemed set to marry when Dave Dexter stepped in.'

The customer's quizzical frown was more than enough encouragement for the barber to carry on with an explanation.

'Dave – well he sort of ordered Tommy to back off, that he was moving in and from now on Ellie was his woman.

'There was a fight in the street. Seems the ranch

6

foreman had to drag them apart. There'd been bad blood between them for a while. The sheriff wanted to throw the pair in jail to cool off but in the end he let them go. Ellie saw all this and she told Tommy to leave her alone but he wouldn't take no for an answer and there were words.

'That should have been the end of it, but Dave got to hear about it and next night they were fighting again in the White Horse Saloon. An hour after, Dave was found down a back alley with Kane kneeling over him with a gun in his hand.'

'Anybody see it happen?'

'Yeah, there were witnesses, swore in court they saw Kane plug young Dave when he was walking away.'

The barber completed the shave and haircut, occasionally adding his own opinion of the killing – Dave was a hothead but he didn't deserve to be gunned down in the back; Kane was a coward and he deserved to hang; just because Ellie Jacobs had thrown him over for Dave, that was no reason to kill him even if it was too much for Tommy – losing out to the Dexters again. Only he killed him, sure enough, and now he was going to hang for it. The whole town would be there to see it happen.

The customer examined his new look in the wall mirror and paid the man.

'So – when's the hanging?'

'Less'n four days. The kid won't live to enjoy another Saturday night. You gonna stick around?'

The stranger didn't answer. Instead he asked, 'Who's the law around town?'

The barber offered another throaty chuckle. 'The law?

If you mean the sheriff that'll be Frank Dolan. But the real law – now that's different. Dolan's one of Jake Dexter's men and he owns just about everything around Rico and about as far as you can see.'

The customer put on his hat. 'You saying that includes the law?'

This time the barber grunted. 'You're a stranger here – so you can say that. Me? I need the custom. And I like the peaceful life.'

The man left the shop and headed for the jailhouse. Less than four days. That's all the time he had to carry out the job he had been given – to find out who had really killed Dave Dexter and so save young Tommy from the noose.

Ben McCabe wondered if he would be able to keep the promise he had made to Tommy's mother.

Frank Dolan was a big man, tall, barrel-chested, a thick greying beard covering much of his round, weatherbeaten face. He wasn't the smiling sort, and was unlikely to greet any visitor with a friendly welcome. When McCabe entered the office he felt he was trespassing. Dolan had his feet up on the desk and was thumbing through a sheaf of papers.

McCabe waited for the lawman to speak, but the man behind the badge stubbornly refused to acknowledge his presence.

'I'd like to see your prisoner,' McCabe said.

'No visitors,' Dolan growled without looking up.

McCabe leaned forward and slowly removed the last sheet of paper from the big man's grasp. It was a Wanted

8

poster offering $500 reward for some young hothead, probably the latest in a line calling himself the Utah Kid. McCabe tossed it to one side.

'That's not very friendly, Sheriff,' he said quietly. 'I'm sure you can do better than that if you try.'

Dolan eyed his visitor warily. He was a tall man, a couple of inches above six feet he reckoned, dark-haired, his square jaw recently shaved, his eyes deep penetrating blue. The sheriff removed his feet from the desk and tilted his chair against the office wall.

Again he studied his visitor before speaking.

'Why do you want to see the kid?'

The manner was churlish but McCabe smiled.

'Family business,' he said politely. 'Between me and young Kane.'

The Rico sheriff was in no mood to soften his hard line approach to McCabe's visit.

'You got a name, mister?'

'The name's Ben McCabe, but, hey, listen, Sheriff. I didn't come here looking for trouble. I just want to pass a message on to the kid. You got a law here that says I can't do that?'

Dolan got to his feet. 'All I know is Mr Dexter said no visitors. That's good enough for me and it's good enough for a stranger called Ben McCabe. Now if you want to see Tommy Kane you should be in the square at nine o'clock in four days. Then you can see him swing.'

He reached out to take Ben's elbow but McCabe moved swiftly away.

'By then it'll be too late. Besides, who's gonna know if you ignore Mr Dexter's orders. I'm not going to tell him

9

and nobody else is going to be around to bleat.' He reached inside his shirt pocket and pulled out a roll of bills.

'What'll it cost me for five minutes with a condemned man? Forty dollars? Fifty? A month's pay for looking the other way for five minutes.'

'Five minutes – that's all you want?' Dolan snatched at the bills.

He told McCabe to remove his gunbelt and reached for the bundle of keys hanging on the office wall, then led McCabe through to the back of the building and the jail-house.

'You got five minutes, McCabe,' he said, and left the visitor in the narrow passage. 'Anybody asks – I wasn't here.'

Tommy Kane was sitting on his bunk in the third cell along the corridor, his head buried in his hands. He looked up as McCabe rattled the bars of his cell to attract his attention. His initial shock turned to a nervous half-smile.

'Ben! What are you doing here?'

McCabe didn't answer immediately. Instead he studied the young man on the bunk.

Six years earlier McCabe had been found close to death near the Kanes' farm after being shot by a bounty hunter and it was Tommy, his young brother and their mother and grandfather who had pulled him through and set him back on the road to recovery.

Now, here he was in the small Arizona town of Rico hoping he could repay that debt, but as he stood in the jailhouse and stared through the bars at the boy turned man, he wondered if he was on the trail of a lost cause.

Was this the same Tommy Kane who had once helped to save his life? Tommy and his young brother Josh had found McCabe lying close to death in a Wyoming creek.

Their mother had nursed him back to health and restored him to a normal life. McCabe had been a man on the run, but it was only after he had proved his innocence did he go back to the Kane farm and renew their friendship. But by the time he returned Tommy was already planning a different future for himself. At the age of sixteen and tired of farming, he had left home in search of his fortune. Their paths had not crossed again. Until now.

'Did you kill him, Tommy?'

The question caught the prisoner by surprise and he hesitated before answering.

'Yes or no, son? That's all I need.'

McCabe had promised Elspeth Kane that he would do his best for her son – but only if the boy was innocent. Elspeth had asked for his help after receiving a wire from Ellie Jacobs telling her that her elder son had been arrested on suspicion of murder and that she was sure he hadn't killed Dave Dexter but things were looking black.

Tommy rose from the bunk. He was unsteady on his feet, a shaking, frightened youth and a pale shadow of the confident boy McCabe had known during his stay of recuperation at the Kane farm.

Tommy gripped the bars of his cell, but did not look McCabe in the eye. Instead, head bowed he stared down at the stone floor.

'I've killed nobody, Ben. I swear it.'

'Then how come they're gonna hang you on Saturday?'

Tommy shook his head and groaned in despair.

'It looked bad, Ben, but as God's my judge, I didn't kill Dave Dexter.'

McCabe felt himself desperate to believe him. 'Tell me about it.' He had heard the barber's story but that was only a summary of the official verdict . . . that Dave Dexter had been shot in the back by Tommy Kane.

Tommy was still only two months into his twenty-first year and was close to tears as he struggled for the words to tell McCabe his story. . . .

For more than a year, life in Rico had been good for Tommy Kane. He had arrived on the eve of his eighteenth birthday, nearly two years after leaving his family farm in Wyoming. In between he had held down a string of different ranch jobs in Colorado and Utah before heading south into Arizona. He had arrived in Rico to learn that Jake Dexter, who owned one of the biggest spreads in the territory was hiring cowhands.

Tommy's experience on the Kane farm and a spell as a trail hand convinced Dexter's foreman to take him on and he quickly settled in to become one of the more trusted workers at the DX Ranch.

He was also one of the most popular of the young breed especially with the youngest of the three Dexter brothers, Dave.

The two youngest members of the DX crew formed a natural bond. Dave's brothers Alec and Buck were more than ten years older than their sibling and the age gap meant they had little in common – not even the same

12

mother. When Tommy Kane rode into town Dave saw a likely sidekick and that is how it started. A friendly rivalry built up as they challenged each other to roping and target-shooting competitions. They were evenly matched which made it all the more interesting, especially for the rest of the cowhands who gambled on the outcome of the contests. Each time it ended in handshakes all round and a few drinks in the saloon.

All was fine between the two young cowboys until Ellie Jacobs entered their lives.

It was the night of the Rico Cattlemen's Ball, an annual party paid for by Jake Dexter and the one occasion when the townsfolk and the ranchers shared a common aim – to enjoy themselves.

Dave and Tommy were in their usual high spirits after a day's drinking and were ready to leave when Tommy spotted the town doctor and his daughter standing by the table laden with food and fruit punch. He nudged his friend in the ribs.

'Who's the pretty girl with the old man?'

Dave Dexter grinned. 'Don't waste your time, Tommy, old friend. That's Doc Jacobs and his daughter Ellie. Doc keeps her on a tight rein and he wouldn't let her come within a hundred feet of some smelly cowhand. I know – I've tried.'

Tommy returned the grin. 'Maybe you haven't tried hard enough.' He brushed the dust from his shirt sleeves. 'Look and you might learn something.'

It was the start of a rapid courtship between Tommy and the doctor's daughter – and the beginning of the decline in the friendship of the two young men.

Dave Dexter rode home alone that night while Tommy walked Ellie to her door with her father never more than a few strides behind. Dave had been right about that, Tommy thought, as the couple chatted about nothing in particular.

They met again after she attended the Sunday service and, as their affections grew and Tommy started to win over the dour, possessive doctor, the roping and shooting contests became fewer.

It was after one such shooting competition for which Tommy showed next to no appetite and lost easily, that Dave challenged his friend full on.

'What's gone wrong with you, Tommy? You sure ain't youself.'

'There's nothing wrong,' Tommy answered sourly, but Dave refused to let it drop.

'You know somethin'? Kelly reckons you ain't pullin' your weight around the ranch these days – says you're spending too much time chasin' after that Jacobs girl to be much use as a cowhand.'

'Ellie, Dave – her name's Ellie and you know it!' He didn't want to sound so aggressive, but he resented foreman Joe Kelly relaying any message he had for him through his close friend. 'Besides, if Joe's got anything to say to me he can say it to my face. He doesn't need to send a messenger boy.'

'Messenger boy? Is that all I am, Tommy? And here was me thinking we were friends. Maybe we were once, but that was before you started walking out with Ellie' – he stressed the use of the girl's name – 'and now I hardly ever see you outside fence fixing and branding. Strikes me,

14

Tommy, Kelly may have something in what he's saying.'

With that he turned and walked away, leaving Tommy staring into the dust and wondering if this was the truth.

Within a week Tommy had left the Dexter ranch to move into town where he worked in the general store and in the livery stable. His courtship of Ellie Jacobs blossomed and within a few weeks they announced their intention to marry.

The paths of the former friends did not cross again until two weeks before the planned wedding. Tommy was leaving the general store when he spotted Ellie and Dave at the corner of the street and from a distance they appeared to be arguing.

As he approached the pair, Dave reached out and grabbed Ellie by the arm. She shook herself free, but he wouldn't let her go. Instead he threw his arms around her and they both stumbled into the street.

As Tommy rushed up to intervene it became obvious that Dave had been drinking. Snatching at the other man's arm, Tommy pulled him away from Ellie but, instinctively, Dave swung a wild punch that caught Tommy flush on the jaw sending him spinning into the dust. Dave stood above him, his fists clenched at his sides but he was unsteady on his feet and Tommy quickly realized that a stand-up fist fight would solve nothing.

Slowly getting to his feet, he rubbed his jaw. 'You're drunk, Dave,' he said calmly. He reached out to calm his friend, but Dexter shrugged free, staggering backwards and almost falling into a horse trough.

But the rumpus was over in a few moments as Dave, cursing as he fell, slumped to the ground in a drunken stupor.

Tommy knelt down to help his friend, but he was stopped when a hand gripped his shoulder and pulled him off.

'You've done enough damage, Kane.'

The voice was a deep-throated snarl and Tommy turned to see ranch foreman Joe Kelly's lined, ravaged face staring down at him.

Tommy got to his feet.

'Hold on, Joe. Dave's drunk and he was annoying Ellie. I haven't touched him. He just fell without any help from me.'

But Dexter's head man shrugged the protest aside.

'I saw what happened. And, yeah, Dave's been drinking and he ain't in any fit state to fight anybody.'

'We weren't fighting, Joe. I was trying to stop him making a fool of himself.'

But Kelly pushed him aside.

'Like I said, Kane – I saw it all. Now, outa my way.'

Another hand tugged at Tommy's sleeve. This time it was Ellie.

'Come away, honey. Let's leave Mr Kelly to sort things out.'

Reluctantly the young couple moved off and watched the ranch foreman help Dave Dexter into the back of a buckboard before driving off out of town.

By the end of the following day the youngest of the three Dexter boys was shot in the back in a dark alley off Rico's main street and Tommy Kane was found kneeling over the body and holding the gun that killed him.

Tommy was fighting to hold back the tears as he told his story.

'I swear, Ben, I didn't kill Dave,' he stammered.

'So tell me.'

'The day after that little ruckus, Dave came into the store to see me. He was sober this time and he wasn't looking for a fight but he was, well, he was reluctant to say too much. He kept looking over his shoulder as though he expected somebody to come bursting in.'

Tommy paused, wringing his hands and pacing across the cell.

'He said he was sorry for the way he had been with me over Ellie and could we go back to the way things were? We even shook hands, but Dave still didn't seem able to relax. When I asked him what was wrong he said he needed to talk and he wanted my help about something. We agreed to meet that night when nobody was around.

'I waited at the bar of the White Horse that night, but when Dave came in it seemed he'd had a few drinks. He staggered up to the bar but when I tried to talk to him he just lashed out, said he'd changed his mind and to keep out of his way. He pushed me over and then ran out.

'I couldn't understand it so I went after him, following him down the street and shouting after him. He turned off at Bonnie's Hat Shop and into the alley.'

'Then . . . tell me what happened.'

Tommy was silent for a few seconds as though he was gathering his thoughts.

'Somebody shot him,' he said simply, his voice little more than a croak. 'I called out his name, but before he could turn round somebody behind me fired two shots. Dave never had a chance. I looked round but didn't see anybody – it was too dark – and when I got to Dave it was

17

too late. He was already dying. Next thing I know the gun that killed him was in my hand and it seemed half the town was standing over us. Whoever had killed Dave hit me from behind. After that – well, I don't know. All I'm sure about is that I didn't kill him.'

Another uneasy silence, then Ben asked, 'What about the gun?'

Again Tommy thought long and hard before replying. 'It was my gun, but I swear, I haven't even worn it since Ellie and I decided to get married. She hates guns, and she had a strong aversion to the sort of people who carry them. To tell the truth, Ben, I haven't felt the need of a gun since I left the DX.'

Suddenly they were interrupted. The door at the end of the corridor burst open and a tall, grey-haired figure in a long-tailed black suit, white shirt and stetson blocked the doorway. He was pointing a six-gun at McCabe's chest.

'Who the hell let you in here? I told Dolan nobody was to speak to that killer.'

Ben turned and knew imediately that he was face to face with the man used to giving orders and getting answers to his questions.

'I guess you must be Jake Dexter. The sheriff was out when I came in. The name's Ben McCabe.'

The tall rancher took a step forward but didn't lower the Colt.

'Then you can just let yourself out again, Ben McCabe. That coward behind those bars killed my son and he's going to hang for it come Saturday.'

Ben edged towards the exit which was still blocked by the cattleman. 'Maybe – maybe not,' he said pushing past.

Grabbing his gun from where he had left it on the office desk, he stepped out into the sunlight. He was nowhere near as confident as he had tried to sound. He believed Tommy, but less than four days might not be enough time to find the real killer of Dave Dexter.

TWO

The sign on the gate swung in the breeze. DOCTOR NOAH JACOBS was in neat white letters on a green board.

It was the right place – a smart, wooden, two-storey house at the end of Main Street surrounded by a well-kept flowerbed that suggested a woman's touch. Ellie Jacobs perhaps.

But it was a man who answered McCabe's heavy knock on the door, a small, round man in a striped, collarless shirt and wearing reading glasses perched on his balding head – every inch the small-town doctor.

'Yes?' There was no smile, no friendly welcome. The town of Rico was clearly short of goodwill among its citizens.

'Doctor Jacobs?'

The man on the doorstep looked his visitor up and down before replying.

'You in need of a doctor?'

McCabe ignored the question. 'I'd like to talk to your daughter, Dr Jacobs. That's if you are Ellie's father.'

'I am. But what do you want with her, Mr. . . .'

'Ben McCabe. I'm a friend of Tommy Kane.'

As soon as he had spoken the name, Ben sensed the man's mood change from cool to openly hostile.

'Then my daughter has nothing to say to you.'

He stepped back inside the house and moved to slam the door in Ben's face, but McCabe was too quick for him, pushing his booted foot over the threshold. A look of alarm appeared on the doctor's flushed face. 'Now, look here—'

'No, Doctor, I don't have time for niceties. I only want to speak to your daughter. Now, is she here?'

The doctor looked terrified.

'Er, no – she's . . . she's. . . .'

Ben smiled but without humour. 'Sorry, Doc – you took far too long over that answer. So, do you let me in peaceful like, or do I get really rough? Remember, I didn't come here to hurt you – just to see Ellie.'

'How . . . how do I know you're not. . . ?'

Ben pushed the door open and stepped inside the house. He reached into the hip pocket of his trousers and pulled out a sheet of notepaper. 'I don't know how much your daughter tells you, Doc, but this is a telegraph she sent to Tommy's mother. I'm what you might call a family friend and she asked me to help. Seems to me like Ellie doesn't think Tommy killed the young Dexter boy.'

He thrust the wire into the doctor's hand. The old man lowered the spectacles from their perch on his domelike head and slowly read the contents.

When he spoke his voice was weary, full of resignation.

'Eleanor told me she was going to wire the young man's family. I pleaded with her not to get involved, to let the law

21

take its course but she wouldn't listen. I told her no good could come of this; that a jury would hear the evidence and decide on Kane's guilt or innocence. That's how it should be, but she argued that this was the man she planned to marry and—'

Ben interrupted him.

'Hold on, Doc – you say they were going to be married?'

'That's right.'

So the barber's version wasn't the whole truth. If his story of Dave splitting them up was wrong, what else was there that didn't fit in with the truth?

Quite suddenly, Doc Jacobs regained his composure and stared Ben in the face.

'I'm sorry, Mr McCabe, you may mean us no harm, but I won't willingly allow you to speak to my daughter. It would only cause her more upset and I can't have that. If, as I am trying to believe, you are an honourable man, you will leave us alone to deal with this.'

Ben folded the message and returned it to his pocket.

'Tell me, Doc, you say Tommy and Ellie were going to be married. How did you feel about that?'

'At first I was sceptical, but I could see he made my daughter happy and she hasn't been that way since her mother died.'

'And do you think Tommy killed Dave Dexter?'

Jacobs answered immediately. 'The evidence was clear. And there were witnesses.'

Ben's smile was almost invisible.

'Thanks, Doc,' he said, turning to leave.

Briefly baffled, Jacobs frowned. 'Thanks. For what exactly?'

'For not answering the question. Tell Ellie I'll talk to her later.'

He left the house and, as he closed the picket gate behind him, he glanced towards the upstairs window just in time to see the lace curtain dropping back into place. Ellie Jacobs watched him walk away and head for the Rico Hotel.

Jake Dexter was in a foul mood. He had called on Frank Dolan to check that nobody had been asking about the Kane kid only to find his puppet lawman was out of the office and a stranger was talking to the prisoner.

'I told you, Dolan – no visitors,' he barked his order, as the sheriff came into the office. He had already prepared his excuse, feeble as it was, it was worth the risk for fifty dollars – a month's pay like the stranger had said.

'I just stepped out to see Lily at the hotel and order in some food. I must have forgotten to lock the door. I'm sorry, Mr Dexter. It won't happen again.'

'See it doesn't, Dolan – I can always get me another sheriff.'

Frank Dolan knew that was true enough. Jake Dexter could engineer a vote just the way he ran almost everything else around Rico.

The cattleman allowed the threat to sink in before adding, 'I want to know all about this McCabe. Where's he from? What does he want, and what's he got to do with Kane? Find out – and if you have got to beat it out of that killer back there – do it!'

He had stormed out of the lawman's office and his mood had not improved by the time he reached the DX.

Maybe it would have been better if Kelly had shot the kid when he spotted him in the alley. He had made a run for it but instead of gunning him down, Kelly had stood back while Buck knocked the kid out and dragged him off to the jail.

Inside the large, sprawling ranch house, Buck Dexter was having a heated argument with his younger brother. As their father entered the room Alec sprang to his feet and lunged at the bigger man. Grabbing his shirt front he tried to pull Buck to the ground, but the older of the Dexter sons swatted him aside.

'Calm down, you two – if you want to fight do it outside!'

Jake brushed past the two brothers and headed for his private office at the back of the house. Lighting himself one of his favourite cigars, the old man strolled out to the rear veranda and stared across the vast landscape that was the DX ranch.

Out to the west a group of ranch hands were rounding up a few head which had strayed from the main herd, but Dexter had little interest in the workings of his ranch these days. The murder of his youngest son had killed any enthusiasm he had left.

Now, in another room, his two eldest boys were quarrelling again. Buck had always been the level-headed one, the son who would eventually inherit the ranch. Alec knew as much and was naturally resentful, living in his brother's shadow.

Their mother had died when they were still boys, but Jake had soon met and married Elizabeth and within a year David was born. Three sons, a happy second marriage, and the biggest ranch in eastern Arizona – more than any man could wish for. But this ideal world had been shattered by a series of disasters ending in the heartache of Dave's death at such a young age.

His own troubles had started little over a year before. At first it was only a stomach pain; he'd had many of those during his life on the trail, caused mainly by bad chuck-wagon food and heavy drinking sessions.

This was different. He ate only fresh meat cooked by Elizabeth and his whiskey drinking was confined to rare social occasions. But the pains became more frequent and intense until he knew that the time had come to see a doctor. Not the Rico man, Jacobs – he would simply offer him more painkiller pills and a lecture on his lifestyle. Dexter knew he needed more and that meant a train journey to one of the territory's major towns – probably even as far as Phoenix. The pretext of a Cattlemen's Convention that needed his attention allowed him a few days away from the DX without arousing Elizabeth's suspicions or worries.

By the time he returned to the ranch a week later Dexter had the information that he had dreaded – that time was running out for him. A spate of rustling on the eastern rim of the ranch had cost him hundreds of head of his prize beef and he had ordered his man Dolan to call in a US marshal to track down the cattle-thieves who had plundered two other ranches in the area. Two of his men who had stumbled across the rustlers' camp had been shot down in cold blood and the cattle-thieves remained free.

The growing tension between Buck and Alec caused him more problems, but he left that in the hands of his foreman. Kelly was in charge of the ranch hands and the brothers were his responsibility.

Then came the death of Dave – gunned in the back by his best friend.

Jake Dexter, hard, ruthless and unbending, a man who ran his business as he ran his life for many years, felt exposed to the weaknesses he had long despised in others. He felt like a man isolated and friendless. Suddenly, however, he was no longer alone. A light rustling sound caused him to turn away from the veranda rail to find Elizabeth at his elbow. Slipping her arm through his she tried to smile but there was only sadness in her eyes.

Her once beautiful features were now pale and thin. Ever since her son's death she had spent the days confined to her room, appearing only for the funeral and the trial of Tommy Kane.

Dexter drew his wife closer, shuddering at the feel of her slender frame as she nestled in his arms.

They stood together in slence, gazing out at the setting sun. Dexter knew the time was coming when he would have to tell Elizabeth of the illness. But not yet, not while she was still grieving for her son.

Ben McCabe re-read the message that Ellie Jacobs had sent to Elspeth Kane. It was clear that Ellie believed Tommy was innocent, but that was hardly enough. He had been found guilty and in four days he would hang unless McCabe could find the real killer. If the story the barber had told him was even close to the truth the whole town believed that the evidence added up to the guilty verdict.

Tommy had denied there had been any fight in the

saloon so that seemed as good a place to start as any, but if Jake Dexter owned the town, as the barber had reckoned, the chances were that all he would get there was confirmation of what he had been told.

And from what he had been told so far, Rico was a town under orders from the DX Ranch.

The saloon was almost deserted, only a handful of early-evening card players occupying the tables when Ben crossed the street from his hotel and entered the dimly lit bar room.

The piano player was tinkering over a tune he didn't recognize and the barman was stacking shelves in readiness for the arrival of the White Horse regulars.

Spotting McCabe, the barman turned on his welcoming smile reserved for a new face and ambled across to greet the newcomer. Ben ordered a beer and waited for the chance to bring up the murder.

'Yeah, I saw the fight,' the barman Ezra Noone chuckled, 'though as fights go it hardly registered – it was more of an argument between two friends. Aren't friends supposed to argue now and agin?'

'So – what happened when the sheriff came?'

Noone let out another of his throaty chuckles. 'Dolan – he never came near the place. Left things like that up to his young deputy. Naw, Dolan's never around when there's any hint of trouble.'

Suddenly, Ezra Noone paused and looked quizzically at McCabe.

'For a stranger in town you seem mighty interested in some little local trouble.'

'I'm told it ended in murder – some little trouble,'

27

McCabe answered trying to sidestep the barman's curiosity.

Noone shrugged. Talking to a stranger made a pleasant change from listening to the locals and their problems all night.

'Dave and young Tommy were arguing about something. Seems they'd had a squabble out in the street the day before. Young Kane came in and said he was waiting for Dave. He wasn't a regular in here and he still had his glass of beer when Dave came back. He had already been in for a spell and he was in an all-fired hurry. They'd hardly spoken a word when Dave lashed out, sending him against the bar and knocking over his beer. He yelled something and there was a bit of a struggle before Dave ran out.

'Tommy got up, brushed himself down and then said something like – "that's what I get for listening to that crazy fool". Then he went off in search of Dave.' He moved to refill McCabe's empty glass. 'Next thing I hear Dave's dead and they've got the kid behind bars for plugging him in the back. Something 'bout a row over young Ellie Jacobs, they said.'

'Was Kane carrying a gun?'

'Who are you, mister? What's with all these questions?'

Ben took a long drink of his beer while he studied the barman's face.

It was a face marked with the ravages of fifty or more hard winter nights and hot summer days but there was something about the twinkle that was still in the deep blue eyes that made Ben wonder . . . was this just another of Jake Dexter's men? Another told to report every move of a stranger asking questions?

'Just curious,' he answered at last. 'Seems strange,

28

gunning down your friend, but I heard there were witnesses to the killing.'

Ezra Noone breathed heavily on the glass he was polishing.

'Look, mister,' he said quietly, moving closer to McCabe, 'seems to me you're more than just a stranger passing through who's interested in a back-alley killing, so you didn't hear this from me. Before Tommy got here, young Dave was telling me—' He stopped in mid-sentence, staring over McCabe's shoulder as the batwing doors sprung open. Ben turned to see who had entered the saloon. Sheriff Frank Dolan was walking towards the bar. Ezra moved swiftly away as though he had been caught out in some treacherous act.

Dolan was grim-faced – exactly the expression Ben remembered – and scowled in the direction of the barman. But it was McCabe he headed towards and, when he reached the bar, the scowl briefly disappeared to become a strange smirk that probably passed for a Dolan smile.

'You look a happy man, Sheriff.' Ben's tone was heavy with sarcasm.

'Could be, McCabe,' Dolan smirked. 'Looks as though you might not have to stay here in Rico as long as you think.' He reached inside his chest pocket and pulled out a sheet of paper.

'Got here a telegraph message. The hangman will be coming in on tomorrow's stage. Seems he's got a lotta business up north and wants to be on his way. He's bringing the hanging forward a couple days. Your young killer friend will swing the day after tomorrow.'

THREE

Ben McCabe paced the floor of his neat hotel room. The news that Tommy Kane would be hanged in two days' time – news delivered with such cynical smugness by the sheriff – had changed everything.

Four days was little enough time to search out a killer in a town where they believed they already had the guilty man behind bars, but now that was down to less than two and McCabe would have to think again.

And he did not like what he was being forced to consider . . . that saving his young friend from the noose might be a promise he could not keep. He spent a restless night ahead of the final day of Tommy Kane's life but it helped him to reach a decision – that if all else failed he would break his young friend out of jail.

An early morning haze was lifting from the dusty streets of Rico when McCabe entered the dining-room at the rear of the hotel. The majority of the tables were empty and McCabe took a seat in the corner before ordering his steak and eggs.

He was not alone for long. He had hardly started his meal when the door leading from the hotel's front hall opened and a young woman entered the room.

Glancing around, she instantly dismissed the young couple at the nearest table and the red-faced diner in the check suit of a salesman. She spotted the man she was looking for in the far corner.

McCabe looked up from his plate as she approached his table. He could see that she was nervous, hesitant and there was a sadness in her pale face.

'Sit down, Miss Jacobs,' he said, rising from his own seat.

'You know who I am?' she asked. He tried a friendly smile.

'More importantly, you know who I am and I can't think of any other young lady in Rico who would feel the urgent need to come and see me over the breakfast table.'

She slid into the chair opposite but did not return the smile. Ellie Jacobs was pretty enough but hers was hardly a face an artist would wish to capture in oils.

'You weren't hard to find, Mr McCabe,' she said quietly. 'I heard you talking to my father yesterday and then saw you heading for the hotel. There are not many good eating places in Rico so this was the obvious place to start.'

She sat silently for a moment and then, in a voice that trembled, she said, 'Tommy didn't kill his friend. Do you believe that?'

'I've read the message you sent to his mother. That is why I'm here. But there is not much time. One day.'

The look of horror on Ellie Jacobs's face was enough to tell McCabe that she knew nothing of the new date for the hanging.

31

She started to sob, dabbing her eyes with a lace hand-kerchief. McCabe reached out and touched her hand.

'Look, I know Tommy didn't kill Dave Dexter, but—' He paused before adding, 'We'll get him out of jail. One way or another – we'll stop the hanging.'

There was a long, uncomfortable silence between them before Ellie said suddenly, 'They lied in court. Those witnesses – they lied.'

McCabe lowered his cutlery.

'Tell me,' he said softly. 'Who lied? Who were the witnesses?'

Ben had already thought about the fact that there had been witnesses to the killing. If somebody was out to kill, then a dark and narrow alley behind a hat shop would make the ideal place. A quiet backstreet hardly used and certainly never in darkness, but on the night of the shooting the alley was almost over-run with men who would swear they saw Tommy Kane gun down the youngest of the Dexter brothers and four of them, all from the DX ranch, had given the evidence that condemned Tommy to the gallows.

Ellie's memories of the trial were delivered hesitantly through a succession of sobs.

'There was Joe Kelly, the foreman, Alec Dexter and two other ranch hands. Buck was with them, but said he didn't see what happened; just that he chased Tommy down and dragged him off to jail.

'It was Kelly who told the court he had been in the White Horse and had seen the two friends arguing. He said he followed them out of the saloon, taking his ranch hands with him because he thought there might be more trouble between the two. He said he got there just ahead of the others to see Tommy pulling the trigger and shooting Dave in the back. The others – including Alec – backed his story, but it was Buck's evidence that persuaded the judge. He was with them but he didn't see what happened – just that he chased after Tommy and caught him holding the gun that killed Dave. It was Tommy's Colt.'

'Damning enough,' McCabe mused barely audibly, but loud enough for Ellie to stiffen.

'Why are you doing this, Mr McCabe?' she asked.

For a reply, McCabe reached inside his shirt pocket and pulled out a bullet. Rolling it between his fingers, he held it out in front of her.

'I keep this as a reminder. Nearly six years ago, Tommy's grandfather took this bullet out of my chest. Another hit me in the head' – he fingered the fading scar on his temple – 'and I was left for dead in a creek near the family's farm in Wyoming. They nursed me back to health and this bullet reminds me of what I owe the family. Someday, if we get him out of this, Tommy will tell you all about it. Till then, let's just say I like to pay my debts.'

He returned the bullet to his pocket and rose from the table.

'What will you do?' Ellie asked.

'First thing, I'm going out to the DX ranch to see the big man around these parts. His son's been murdered and I think he'll want to be sure that they are hanging the right man.'

Ellie Jacobs touched his arm. 'Is there anything I can do?'

McCabe smiled and said, 'I hope not, Ellie. If I need

your help it will mean that I haven't found the real killer. . . .'

Jake Dexter winced at the sharp stabbing pain in his stomach. He was standing on the veranda of the DX ranch house and watching a lone rider approaching from eastern ridge that bordered the spread and separated it from the small town of Rico.

The stranger was well within hailing distance before the cattleman recognized him as the prying stranger whom Dolan had allowed into the cells to talk to young Kane. What the hell could he want here? Dexter wondered, turning towards the house.

'Buck!' he called. 'Come on out here – I might need you!'

The man who came out of the house was a couple of inches shorter than his father but there was no mistaking the bloodline.

They stood shoulder to shoulder and watched McCabe dismount, hitch his horse to a rail near the corral and stride purposefully towards them. Old man Dexter went down the steps to meet him.

'What are you doin' out here, McCabe – I said all I had to say to you in the jail.'

'Dolan will have told you the new day for the hanging,' Ben said. 'It's tomorrow.'

Dexter remained unmoved. 'You didn't have to come out here to tell me. I'm not interested when Kane hangs – just that he does.'

The old man turned to go back up the steps.

'He didn't kill your son, Mr Dexter,' Ben said quietly.

'Hanging Tommy Kane won't give you your killer.'

Buck stepped forward and made his way down the steps.

'Listen, Mr McCabe – whoever you are – I don't know what that kid's been telling you. He killed Dave and there were enough witnesses. I was there.'

'And did you see the shooting?'

'I caught the kid with the gun in his hand. Joe Kelly saw the shooting. And two of the ranch hands.'

'And Alec,' the old man interrupted. 'My son saw his young brother gunned down in that alley, McCabe. So don't come to my house crying for some killer.' His voice was rising and had almost reached a scream when the old man suddenly stiffened and let out a yell of pain.

McCabe dashed forward and caught the ranch owner, stopping him from collapsing into the dust.

Buck was quickly at his side and together the pair helped the cattleman into the house.

'Over here!' Buck ordered, edging towards a couch in the corner.

Jake Dexter groaned as he was lowered on to the seat.

'What's wrong with him?' Buck sensed there was genuine concern in the stranger's question but he simply shrugged.

'He doesn't talk about it, says it's just—' They were interrupted when a pale, slightly built woman came into the room. Buck spun round as she gasped at the sight of the man on the couch.

'Elizabeth!'

She ignored him and hurried across to kneel at the side of her stricken husband.

'What happened?' she asked, her voice scarcely more than a croak.

'He collapsed out on the steps when we were talking to this man,' Buck explained. 'We were just talking when he fell forward and McCabe here managed to catch him.'

She looked up at her stepson and then quickly away. Jake had never spoken about his illness and she could only guess at the seriousness of it. She knew the pain had got worse over the past few months and he was taking more and more painkillers. She had heard him pacing the floor late in to the night but she dared not ask him. She dared not face up to the fears of what the answer would bring.

'Thanks for your help, Mr McCabe, but I'd like you to leave us alone now.' She turned back towards her husband and Buck took McCabe's elbow and led him from the room and back out on to the veranda. 'I don't know what you expected to find here, McCabe,' Buck said, as they reached the bottom of the steps, 'but Tommy Kane was found guilty of Dave's murder on the evidence of four witnesses – including my brother, Alec. My father's got other things to worry about than the fate of his son's killer.

'We've had big problems with rustlers who killed two of our hands less than a month ago. And there's Alec . . . look, McCabe, maybe I shouldn't be talking to you, but it's only right that you should know how things work around these parts.

'Tommy got a fair trial – my father saw to that. He may be hard and cold-blooded at times, but he's fair. You can ask anybody in Rico—'

Ben tried to hold back a sneer. 'Come on, Dexter, your father owns Rico – I've already learned that much. I came out here to try to save an innocent kid's life and all I get is a story of rustlers and killings and the problems of the DX Ranch.

'Who were the other witnesses? Your foreman Kelly – who else?'

'Zeb Maddox and a Canadian, Moose – I don't remember his name.'

'And your brother, Alec,' Ben reminded him.

'Listen, McCabe, leave Alec out of this. He might not have got on too well with his stepbrother, or Kane, but he said what he saw.'

Buck's voice was rising in anger but he managed to control himself and softened his approach.

'I didn't think young Tommy was capable of killing Dave. They were friends until Kane took up with Ellie Jacobs.'

'That's what I heard,' Ben said, 'except Tommy doesn't agree. He said Dave wanted to see him that night – that he had something important to tell him. That doesn't sound like they'd had a big fall-out, does it?'

When Buck didn't answer Ben pressed on, 'I guess you don't know what Dave wanted to talk about?'

Again only a shake of the head came as a reply.

Ben put on his hat and moved to leave. 'Hope your father's up and about soon.'

'Thanks,' said Buck trying to raise a smile, 'and if you're still looking for Zeb Maddox or Moose you'll likely find them down on the southern pasture fixing fences. Though, like I said, you're wasting your time.'

Ben mounted up, touched his hat and headed back towards town. It was too late to challenge the DX

37

witnesses. It was time to think of a way of arranging a jail break. After that they would have time to find the real killer and clear Tommy's name.

But he didn't make it back to Rico before running into the sort of trouble that convinced him Tommy Kane was innocent.

FOUR

There were three of them side by side across the track leading out of the DX Ranch. The middle man of the three riders blocking McCabe's path nudged his horse slowly forward. He was a narrow-shouldered man with dark, hooded eyes set close together, an aquiline nose and hollow cheeks. He wore a three-day growth of beard that was turning to grey. He leaned forward on the horn of his saddle. Behind him the others sat bolt upright, their right hands menacingly close to their holsters.

McCabe tensed. There was not a friendly face among the trio and when the man spoke there was nothing friendly in his voice.

'We hear you've bin stirrin' up trouble and we ain't too happy about that.' His companions nodded their agreement.

McCabe studied the men. He reckoned he could probably take down two of them if it came to a shoot-out, but the chances of getting all three were not worth taking. He stayed silent.

The thin man shifted in his saddle.

'Looks like we got the quiet type here, boys.'

The others grinned.

' 'Cept he ain't been quiet enough. That right, McCabe?'

So they knew who he was and they must have known why he was at the Dexter spread. He decided it was time to play his own hunch.

'You must be Kelly, the foreman. And one of these apes is Moose.'

He paused then added, 'I can guess which – he'll be the one whose horse is near to buckling under him.'

For the first time the thin man's expression changed and the movement almost resembled a smile.

'And the ugly one's Zeb Maddox, so now we're all acquainted. We've been watching you, McCabe, ever since that sheriff Dolan let you in to talk to the kid. Now we reckon you've been to see the old man trying to convince him that Kane didn't kill young Dave.'

'You seem to know a lot, Kelly. Thing is, I don't think young Tommy did kill his friend.'

Kelly turned again in his saddle.

'You hear that, boys? Mr McCabe here is calling us all liars. Says we didn't tell the judge the truth about that night. We told what we saw and the Kane kid gunned down young Dave sure enough.'

McCabe was prepared for what happened next, but there was nothing he could do about it. All three drew their Colts and pointed them at his chest. But they weren't going to kill him. If they had killing in mind they would not have hung around to introduce themselves. Shooting him there – out in the open when anybody could pass by

40

– would be stupid and they were not stupid. And they would have to explain away his body to their boss.

'Drop your gunbelt and get out of your saddle, McCabe. And do it easy. We're going for a little walk.'

Ben did as he was ordered and the man called Maddox trotted his horse up and took the reins of McCabe's mount. Nobody spoke as they made their way into a deep undergrowth. Ahead was a small, derelict shack. But McCabe never made it. Without warning, he was felled by a vicious blow from behind, a gun-butt sending him into oblivion. As blackness enveloped him Ben was aware only of the voice of the man called Kelly barking out his orders to the others.

The room was in total darkness and Ben McCabe was alone, tied and gagged. As consciousness returned and his eyes became accustomed to the lack of light, he could make out a pot-bellied stove, a small table and chair and a bunk bed set against the far wall. If there were any windows they were boarded and there was just a single door to his left. The ropes dug into his wrists and ankles and his arms were stretched to wrap around the back of a chair. His head ached from the blow that had laid him unconscious.

For several minutes McCabe sat motionless to think about his predicament. He had no idea how long he had been in the abandoned shack, but he had no difficulty in figuring out why he was there. Kelly – or whoever was giving him his orders – wanted him out of the way.

Not permanently – they could have put a bullet in him and few people would have asked questions about a

41

missing stranger. They wanted to keep him out of Rico and block his chances of asking more tricky questions. Kelly had sneered at the suggestion that Tommy might not have been the killer.

'*You hear that, boys? McCabe here's calling us all liars. We told what we saw and the Kane kid gunned down young Dave sure enough.*'

Ben remembered Kelly's contempt and the smirk on the face of the others. But had they seen the killing? Or was Tommy a convenient stooge? McCabe wrestled with the thought but only briefly. If Tommy hadn't killed young Dexter it meant somebody else had and Kelly and his men were hiding something.

Trapped in the shack, Ben could do nothing. He had to find a way to free himself, to get back into Rico and, he realized, that the only way of saving Tommy from the noose now was to break him out of jail. Kelly had clearly figured that there was no necessity to guard an unarmed man tied and gagged in a deserted shack some five hours' walk outside of town. He had already rendered the prying stranger harmless.

McCabe peered into the gloom of the shack hoping to see something – a knife, broken glass – anything that could assist his escape. There was nothing . . . except above a small sink near the door, a mirror on the wall.

Slowly, he edged across the room and then forced himself to crash to the floor in an effort to smash the flimsy framework of the chair to which he was tied. It needed three painful attempts before he finally heard the crack of the wood as one of the chair legs gave way. Another fall and his arms were free of the broken chair.

Gradually, he was able to climb awkwardly on to the sink and kick the mirror from its nail in the wall. His luck was in, the mirror fell on to the stone floor of the shack and shattered into pieces.

Groping around in the darkness, his hands still firmly tied behind his back, McCabe eventually found a piece of the mirror glass large enough to use as a cutting tool and work on the ropes binding his wrists.

It was slow and painful, twice he felt the glass cut into his skin and the blood on his fingers, but eventually the slow and painstaking effort was successful and he broke free.

Rubbing his wrists and washing his bleeding hands in the cold water from a jug at the side of the sink, McCabe soon turned his attention to the next obstacle between him and freedom. The locked door.

A search of the shack produced the perfect tool, a discarded branding iron. Using it to smash through the lock and splintering the wood around it, he was free in a matter of minutes.

But as he stepped out into the cold air he knew instantly that time was against him.

He was stranded in a remote area of a vast ranch twenty or more miles away from where he needed to be. And although he had no idea of the hour, the moon was high in the clear Arizona sky. Within the next few hours, Tommy Kane would be dead.

The young prisoner stood on his bunk, gripped the bars of the high window and stared out into the clear moonlit night.

He felt hopelessly alone. Ben McCabe had said he would do everything he could to fight for his freedom. But where was he? Why had he not returned to the jail like he had promised?

Dejectedly, Tommy slumped on to the bunk, sat with his knees up to his chest and his arms wrapped around his legs.

He was barely twenty years old. Too young to die for a crime he did not commit. He felt the tears welling up in his eyes and he started to pray. He had not done that since he was a boy and they had buried his father, a town marshal, shot down by a drunken cowboy.

Now he was crying for his own life. Where was Ben McCabe?

The road between the DX Ranch and the town of Rico was little better than a well-worn track littered with holes and fallen rocks and McCabe was grateful for the light of the moon. But it was still slow and tiring and his head ached from the blow of Kelly's gun butt.

Twice he slipped into a ditch but knew he could stop only briefly to regain his breath before moving on. He had no idea how long his trek from the shack took him, but by the time he reached the outskirts of town and passed the ghostly skeleton of the newly erected gallows, fatigue was getting the better of him. He had used the long, exhausting hours of the journey to formulate a plan of action.

The darkened windows of the homes, stores and saloons confirmed his hope that the good citizens of Rico were still in their beds so the first part of McCabe's plan would be no problem.

His first stop was at the town's general store and gun-smith's where he easily forced the feeble lock. He noticed the name of Dexter over the door so felt a sense of moral justice in what he was about to do. Once inside he raided the cabinets for six-guns, belts and a rifle before searching through the drawers for cartridges, pausing occasionally to listen for any break in the silence from the rooms upstairs. The Dexter family might own the business but they were sure to have a live-in store manager to run it.

He buckled on a gunbelt, threw the other over his shoulder and checking that there was no immediate evidence of a break-in, made his exit into the back street.

Dodging through the shadows, McCabe edged his way to the far end of town where he knew there was a stable yard and livery.

In order to save young Tommy Kane from the noose, Ben McCabe, lawman and one-time railroad detective, was about to become a horse thief.

FIVE

Dawn was ready to break over the eastern ridge and there was a lamp on in the sheriff's office.

McCabe peered through the window. Sheriff Dolan was nowhere to be seen but his chair was occupied by a young deputy, slumped over the desk apparently dozing.

McCabe gripped the door handle, turned it slowly and silently entered the office. Easing his gun from its holster he crept up behind the young man at the desk. He pressed the barrel of his Colt against the deputy's temple.

'Don't do anything you'll be sorry for,' he whispered, as the startled lawman suddenly froze. 'We don't want to be leaving any dead heroes.' The deputy tried to nod his head and mumbled what McCabe took to be an agreement.

'Let me have the keys to the cells and you'll be fine.'

The young man shook his head. 'I-I can't.'

'Don't be a fool, sonny.'

'No – you . . . you don't understand. I don't have any keys. They're not here. Sheriff Dolan took them with him. He's got them.'

The kid was frightened.

'What's your name, son?'

'D-Danny – Danny Lockwood.'

'Well, Danny Lockwood. How old are you?'

'I'm twenty.'

'Same age as young Tommy back there. You have something else in common too, Danny. If you don't come up with those keys, neither of you will see twenty-one. Tommy will hang for a murder he didn't commit and you – well, you'll die for nothing except to keep Dolan happy.'

McCabe was bluffing, but the young deputy didn't know that.

'Now – where are the keys – and not where the sheriff told you to say they are?'

Ben could sense by the young deputy's hesitation that he needed further prompting.

'Ask yourself, is it worth it? Would Frank Dolan take a bullet for you?' Reluctantly, Danny got to his feet, crossed the office and removed a bunch of keys from a small wall cupboard.

'We always keep a spare set. And, no – I reckon he wouldn't,' he said at last and tossed the keys to Ben. 'And besides, I reckon you may be right about that kid back there. Doesn't seem like the killer type to me.'

Ben offered a thin smile. 'You're a better judge than most people in this town, son. Even so, I need to take precautions. Don't want you runnin' off to find the sheriff as soon as we are out of here.

'So – if you'd just like to change places with Tommy.'

Together they walked through to the jailhouse. Tommy was on his feet gripping the bars of his cell when the pair

47

made their way along the narrow passageway.

Within minutes, the young deputy was locked in his cell and the two men on the run had left by the rear door before Ben hurled the keys into a nearby shrubbery.

It was almost daylight when they left the town of Rico behind them and headed for the only place Ben knew he could get some answers: the DX Ranch.

But first he had to find somewhere he would not be disturbed. He needed to catch up on some lost sleep.

The sign was worn and faded but just about readable, MAC'S TRADING POST.

'Seems as good a place as any to rest up,' Ben said, studying the small wooden building, the one-horse corral and the water trough that made up the stagecoach stopover.

They had been in the saddle for almost three hours and they had ridden hard with barely a word passing between them. The sun was high in the clear sky and the horses needed rest and water.

Ben had spent a long time thinking about what he could do next. Getting Tommy out of jail was the easy part; keeping him out now that he was also on the run and facing the rope as a horse-thief was going to be a lot tougher.

Dolan was sure to organize a posse and if they eventually tracked down the fugitives there would be no such formalities as a trial, Ben and Tommy would face a lynch mob.

'You sure this is a good idea, Ben?' There was alarm in Tommy Kane's voice as the pair eased their horses towards the hitching rail outside the trading post.

Ben chuckled.

'Not if you're going to act as guilty as sin if anybody looks sideways at you. But don't worry, I don't think you're notorious enough to be known at every outpost in the territory. There's a good chance that Mac, whoever he is, wouldn't know you from Jesse James.'

They dismounted and went inside.

An old man was raking over the embers of dead fire and turned at the sound of heavy footsteps on the wooden floor.

'Hi there, strangers,' he said, rising to his full height which took him level with Ben's chest. 'Charlie McDonald at your service. What can I get you?'

'Well, Charlie McDonald, we've been on the road all night and could do with something to eat and hot coffee if it's not too much trouble.'

Charlie McDonald chuckled, a hoarse throaty sound that was a result of too much tobacco chewing and too much coarse whiskey.

'Trouble? Hell, apart from the weekly stage you're the first folks I've seen in nearly a month. I was beginning to think the world had ended, or else the Apaches had taken over.' He giggled. 'Eggs, steak and beans and some of my own baked bread coming up.'

The news that nobody other than the stage had passed his way for nearly a month brought an immediate change in Tommy's mood. He even smiled.

'That would be fine, Charlie.'

'Gimme ten minutes.' With that the old man hobbled out of the room and into the back of the building.

49

Tommy waited until McDonald was well out of earshot before leaning closer. His voice was barely more than a whisper.

'I haven't had chance to thank you for breaking me out, Ben. I was getting to thinking you may have given up on me.'

'A lot has happened since I saw you, Tommy. But we haven't finished yet – not if you want to marry than girl of yours.'

Tommy was silent for a time before he said, 'There's nothing I want more, but it's not going to be. Ellie's not going to marry a man on the run and I wouldn't ask her.'

'So, is that what you're planning? Life on the run – back to Wyoming?'

Tommy shook his head. 'I don't know.'

Ben straightened up. 'Well, here's how I see it, son. You and your family once saved my life so I owe you. And breaking you out of jail doesn't repay the debt. It doesn't even go halfway. You didn't kill Dave Dexter so the only way you can marry Ellie is for us to clear you and that means finding the real killer.'

He paused, then went on, 'What do you know about Joe Kelly and the Dexters?'

'Kelly is Jake Dexter's ranch foreman. Not my kind of guy, mean-spirited, though he treated me well enough when I was at the DX. Not like Alec Dexter. He's bad all through. Beats up on the weak and it's only Joe who can keep him out of real trouble when the boys are in town.

'The older brother, Buck, he's the straightest one in the family – him and Dave.' He paused. 'Hell, Ben, why would anybody kill Dave? He was just a regular, fun-loving young

50

kid.' Tommy slumped in his chair. 'And why would anybody want me to hang for it?'

'I've been thinking about that,' Ben said softly. 'Maybe it had something to do with what Dave was going to tell you. You have no idea what it was?'

Tommy shook his head. 'Guess we'll never know.'

They sat in silence until Charlie returned with their food and coffee.

'You fellas travellin' far?'

It was a question simply to make conversation but instinctively Tommy stiffened.

'Colorado,' Ben said. 'Or Kansas. Maybe Texas.'

Charlie let out one of his throaty chuckles. 'Right, mister. Not my business, huh?'

'You're a good cook, Mr McDonald. Better stick with that.'

He left them alone again, muttering something about the only visitors he ever got were an unfriendly pair of drifters.

They finished the meal in silence, washed it down with more coffee before Ben decided that it was time to draw up some sort of plan.

When he had finished, Tommy felt for the first time since the escape that he had a chance of clearing his name and marrying Ellie Jacobs.

He should have known that Ben would not let him down, but, as the two men rode away from the trading post, neither of them could have guessed what lay ahead.

There were four of them, sheltering from the searing heat of the afternoon sun. They had been waiting since noon and they were growing impatient. The tallest of the trio looked again at his pocket timepiece and grunted another few words of disapproval.

He and his men did not like to be kept waiting.

Suddenly the mood changed for the better. The young one – blond haired, round-faced and stockily built – spotted it, the moving cloud of dust down in the valley.

'He's here!'

The men dismounted, tied their horses to a handy bush and moved towards the edge of the ridge to follow the movements of the approaching rider.

The tall one lowered his spy glass and grunted again. 'It's him. And he's alone.'

The minutes passed as the lone rider made his way up the steep slope, his horse struggling to keep its legs from slipping away from under him. Eventually the gradient became more gradual and when they reached the summit both man and horse were drenched in sweat.

'You're late,' the tall man said, as the new arrival dismounted and took a long drink from his canteen before offering his tired mare the chance to quench its thirst from his Stetson.

'We've had trouble,' the newcomer said, slowly regaining his breath. 'The kid has broken out of Rico jail.'

The tall man grinned crookedly.

'So, no hanging today.' He was a man of few words.

'No, and it means we have to put off our next bit of business.'

The tall man paused in the midst of lighting a fresh cigar. His crooked grin remained in place.

'The kid's your problem, not ours. We've got a deal.'

The newcomer shrugged. 'Nothing I can do. Dolan's got up a posse and his men could be all over the place. We can't move until he's tracked down the kid and the man who got him out of the jail.'

'Like I said – that's for you to worry about.'

The other man mopped his brow, turned and looked out across the wide valley below. He had expected this. The man was a jackass.

'I'm here to give you the message. You know what to do if you don't like it.' he said.

'*I* don't,' the tall man growled. 'You think about it, sonny. We'll give you a day. After that' – he threw down his half-smoked cigar – 'the deal is off and you're out.'

The four mounted up and moved to leave but the newcomer grabbed the reins of the tall man's horse.

'Before you go, thought you might like to know something.' He paused for effect. 'The man who helped the kid escape from Rico jail, he's an old friend of yours; leastways you've cussed him enough since I've known you.

'The name's McCabe. Ben McCabe. Didn't you tell me you put two bullets in him and he lived to talk about it?'

Six years . . . six long years since McCabe had marched Jay Munroe down the main street of Charlsburg, Wyoming to face trial for the murder of a saloon singer. . . .

Munroe's twisted grin had no trace of humour as he recalled how he beat the law and walked free from the courthouse. A pity, he reflected, that McCabe had not stayed around for the trial; he would have learned that nobody tries to make a fool of Jay Munroe and lives to tell the tale.

Sure, he had plunged a knife into that treacherous bitch Carla, but there were no witnesses. Just as there were no witnesses to the shooting of his double-dealing partner Mitchell Dredge, or the shooting of Ben McCabe. Maybe it was a mistake that he had not hung around long enough to finish the job. But now, it looked as though he would get the chance to do that – even if it was almost six years late.

Back then Munroe had been what he still was – a gambling, ladies' man with a heart of stone.

Crooked railroad boss Mitchell Dredge had framed McCabe for robbery and murder and had paid Munroe a $2,000 bounty to kill him. But McCabe had recovered, hunted him down for the killings of Dredge and the saloon singer who had been his mistress, Carla Blake.

Now, some spoiled kid tells him that McCabe is still around.

Next time it would be different . . . Munroe would make sure there was no mistake. Ben McCabe was a dead man walking.

Jake Dexter pushed the half-eaten meal across the table, rose from his chair and looked angrily at his visitor. He turned to his wife and, controlling his growing fury, he said quietly, 'Leave us, Elizabeth, we have business to discuss.'

Elizabeth Dexter knew from long experience that when her husband talked of business it was no place for a wife, however loving and supportive, and the man who had just arrived was not the sort of person she would willingly welcome into her home. The sooner Jake could deal with that this matter the happier she would be.

Dexter waited until she had left the room and he could speak freely. His eldest son, Buck stood at his side as he faced the man wearing the tin star. The old man was fighting to contain his anger.

'You're a fool, Dolan. A brainless fool, leaving a young deputy to guard my son's killer.'

The sheriff knew better than to try to defend himself. He knew from recent experience that an angry Jake Dexter was not a man to cross.

'I want him found. Take as many men as you need off the ranch – but get that Kane kid back.' He tried to hide the effects of another sharp stomach pain by slumping into his chair.

'I'll make it easier for you, Dolan,' he continued, after a brief pause. 'There's a five-thousand-dollar share-out for your posse to bring him in – and I don't care if he's dragged along feet first. Dead or alive, Dolan. I want that killer of my son and if' – another stabbing pain caused him to wince – 'if I can't see him hang I can sure as hell see him buried. Now get out of here while you can still walk.'

Sheriff Dolan turned and hurried out of the house.

Gasping for breath, Dexter staggered slowly to his feet. Leaning heavily on his son's shoulder, the rancher coughed violently. The time had come when he had to tell his family the truth – that his sickness would claim him sooner rather than later.

'Where's Alec?' he croaked, catching the look of alarm on his eldest son's face.

Buck Dexter neither knew nor cared about the whereabouts of his younger brother. Alec was a rebel who went his own way and contributed next to nothing to the running of the DX. But he wasn't going to tell his sickly father his feelings.

'He's out on the range someplace – said he had some business. Probably fixing some of those fences on the north side.'

The old man smiled knowiingly.

'Don't try to fool me, Buck,' he said quietly. 'I know Alec's not the working type. He ain't fixin' fences. But don't you be too hard on him. I suppose it's my fault. I tended to give him everything he wanted when he wanted it. Until. . . .'

His voice tailed off and he spluttered into another coughing fit. He didn't have to finish the sentence – Buck knew that he was going to say.

Until their mother died and the old man married Elizabeth and Dave eventually came along.

'I need him back here, son. Go and find him and bring him home. We . . . we need to talk. All the family. Together.'

Buck Dexter studied the old man. He was a shadow of the figure who had built up the DX Ranch from next to nothing, the man who had been responsible for dragging Rico up from a shanty tent camp into a blossoming Arizona town. True, he had not always been popular; he had trodden on a few sensitive toes to get what he wanted and there were still traces of the power-hungry cattleman in the failing sixty-five-year-old frame. But he had been a good father to Buck and Alec and to Dave – especially to Dave who was his by Elizabeth. Olivia Dexter had been his own mother, but she had died of an illness that now seemed to be overwhelming the old man.

Buck was no fool. He knew that his father was dying, a slow, painful death and he also knew that time was running out. Jake had never before asked to see the family all in one place at the same time. Not since he and Alec were boys and their mother was dying. Now his time was coming and he wanted his family at his side.

'I'll go find Alec and bring him home, Pa,' he said quietly. 'You go through and have some rest.'

Alec Dexter was not fixing fences or rounding up strays. He was not even on the DX ranch. He had carried out the first of his self-imposed assignments – to tell Munroe and the others about the escape from Rico jail; that should take care of the young Kane once and for all – and now he sat at the top of a ridge two hours' ride out of range of the DX hands. He was settling down for another rendezvous, far more important than his morning meeting with the others.

Alec had always known that his life would never follow the same path as his older brother's. Buck was an honest, hard-working man, ideally suited for life on a ranch. Alec chuckled at the thought that he had often had over the years. If Buck hadn't been born a Dexter he would have been born wearing a sheriff's badge, or an army captain's uniform. He was born to be one of life's good guys.

He had always been the favourite son. Tall, broad-shoul-dered, a handsome figure of a man in contrast to Alec's pale face and slight frame – as physically different as it was possible for two brothers to be.

All through their younger days Buck had felt it was his

duty to fight Alec's battles. But those days were long gone.

Even Dave had rated higher in the old man's affections. But now he was gone, too. From now on things would be different. Dexter may have been one of the most powerful names in the territory, but by the time he had finished Alec would make it the most feared as well. And to hell with Buck; to hell with the old man and that feeble-minded stepmother. Below him the valley stretched way to the south from where he knew they would come. They had no use for the gold, or the cash, or the trinkets they would collect for their morning's work. Nor would they flinch at the sight of blood.

What they wanted were rifles. Good, reliable weapons. And that was what Alec Dexter could offer the band of renegades who were determined to avenge a massacre at Camp Grant. Alec had no sympathy for the Apaches, but they served his purpose. He would show Buck and his father and that woman that he could make it alone. He didn't need them. . . .

Ben McCabe stirred from a heavy sleep, lifted himself on to one elbow and stared around the greenery that formed the picture-book glade they had chosen as a place to rest.

Refreshed, McCabe got to his feet and ambled towards the creek.

His horse was lapping at the water. His horse. Not Tommy's. Not Tommy himself.

McCabe swilled his face, stretched his aching limbs and looked around for any sign of young Kane. There was none. Reluctantly, he knew he had to face up to the fact that the friend he had sprung from the Rico jail that very morning, had gone.

Although a scowl of annoyance crossed his face Ben knew that it would be harsh to blame the boy for running off. He was a fugitive, on the run for the murder of one of the town's popular young men and it was only natural that he would want to put a lot of territory between himself and his pursuers. Even so. . . .

'The damn fool kid,' Ben snapped. 'Damn fool!'

But still he was worried and disappointed. Had Tommy ridden off out of fear? Or guilt? He hoped – and still wanted to believe – that young Kane was innocent of the killing of Dave Dexter in the alley that night and he had promised to find the real killer. But now he was not so sure. His young friend's disappearance left him wondering whether he too should head off, maybe back to Wyoming. There was nothing for him here, now, not even if he found the real killer.

He reached down, lifted the reins of his horse and pre-pared to mount up. It was time to ride out. But he got no further.

'Stay right where you are, mister. And don't try any-thing fancy.'

McCabe let the reins drop and spun round. He was staring into the barrel of a rifle pointed at his chest. Holding the weapon was a tall, slender figure with a face that McCabe thought at first sight belonged to the pretti-est woman he had ever seen.

Ben McCabe weighed up the situation. The young woman behind the rifle looked deadly serious and he was not going to take any chances that the finger on the trigger might develop an itch. He released the reins and moved cautiously away from the horse that happily returned to the creek. Ben raised his arms in a token gesture of surrender.

'Take it easy, miss. We don't want any accidents.'

The young woman didn't return the friendly smile.

'It won't be any accident,' she said icily, ordering McCabe into full view. 'Who are you, mister? And what you doin' on my land?'

McCabe relaxed. She didn't know who he was which was reassuring.

'Your land?' he said, trying to sound surprised. 'I thought this was open range and I just stopped to water the horse. Water's still free in these parts, isn't it?'

She ignored the jibe. 'Where you headed?'

Ben shrugged. 'Nowhere special, just passing through.'

The answer seemed to puzzle the woman and Ben lowered his arms and stepped forward. 'I'm not bringing you any trouble, miss.'

Slowly, as though she was still not wholly convinced, the young woman relaxed without encouraging the stranger to think that she would not pull the trigger if he came too close.

'You're not one of Dexter's men?' It was more of a question than a statement and for the first time, Ben knew that the woman was no threat.

'I'm not one of Dexter's men. But supposin' I was – what then?'

For the first time the woman's features broke into a half-smile.

'I'd probably use this first and ask questions after.'

Ben was intrigued.

'Bad blood, huh?'

She didn't answer at first. Instead she studied the tall stranger more closely. She liked what she saw. Broad-shouldered, dark features bordering on her idea of handsome, clear blue eyes and a face that suggested honesty. But handsome features and a winning smile were no guarantees that this man lived his life on the side of the good guys. She felt her grip on the rifle slacken, but as the stranger took a step towards her she quickly regained her resolve.

'I think you ought to mount up and ride out of here, mister. My beef with the Dexters is no concern of yours.'

Ben shrugged. 'I could make it my business – that's if you're looking for some hired help.'

Again the woman was silent. Why should she trust a complete stranger? And why would he offer to help a woman who might just decide to blow his brains out at any moment? She kept the gun pointed squarely at the man's chest.

'What's your name, mister?'

Ben chuckled. 'Now, if I told you that you'd know more about me than I know about you. Let's just say I also have an interest in the Dexters.' He waited. 'Right – I'm Ben McCabe.'

There was no flicker of recognition in the woman's face. She didn't know the name.

'I'm Mollie Cooper, and, like I said, you're trespassing on my land.'

Ben tried to turn on he charm. 'And here was me thinking that Jake Dexter owned every acre east of Phoenix.'

61

It was the woman's turn to smile – a warm smile that reached right up to her eyes, Ben noticed.

'He wishes – but there are still enough of us small ranchers around that he just can't buy out.'

She lowered the rifle. Maybe it was time to take a chance on this man, McCabe. 'You know old man Dexter?'

'We've met,' Ben said.

'Then you'll know he likes to think he owns just about everything around here from the law in Rico all the way down to the general store.'

There was bitterness in the woman's voice.

'And does he?'

Mollie sighed. 'Mostly.' Then she added as an after-thought. 'But the Dexters aren't all bad. The oldest son, Buck, he seems to be a fair-minded, pleasant enough critter. Not like his younger brother Alec and now that Dave's gone—'

'Dave?'

'Dave Dexter. He was the youngest. Half-brother to the other two. He was shot down a couple of weeks back. They arrested some kid for it, a cowhand who used to work for the Dexters. They're due to hang the poor kid some day soon. If you'd have come through Rico you'd have heard all about it.'

'I've heard,' Ben said quietly. 'Except that what I've heard isn't quite what I'm supposed to hear, I reckon.'

She gave him a puzzled look but Ben chose to ignore it. Mollie didn't need to know anything about him and what she didn't know could not cause her any grief.

'So, what's your problems with the DX Ranch then?' he asked after a pause. 'Anything I can do to help?'

Mollie lowered the Springfield and studied the stranger again. Why would he want to help her? Sure, it was tough being a young woman running a ranch – even one as small as the Cooper spread. But so far her feud with the Dexters was nothing she couldn't handle. 'It's a long story you may not want to hear,' she said eventually. Ben thought for a moment. Tommy had gone; he was on the run from the law in Rico and that, he knew, meant he was on the wrong side of the Dexters, and somewhere among the DX crew was the truth behind the killing of young Dave Dexter.

'You could always try me out,' he suggested, climbing into the saddle, 'and show me around your place.'

'Easy, boy, easy.'

Tommy's voice was scarcely more than a whisper. Slowly, silently, he led the horse from its grazing ground close to the creek. A few yards away, Ben stirred briefly from his heavy sleep, rolled on to his side but didn't waken.

Tommy had thought long and hard about his next move – to make his break when the chance came. It was true that he had reason to be grateful to Ben for breaking him out of jail but, as the older man had said more than once, he was only repaying a debt he owed to the Kane family who had saved his life. So Tommy felt no guilt about what he was planning to do. Ben McCabe didn't need him – and now he didn't need Ben. It was time for the pair to part company.

Ben had said he wanted to find the truth behind Dave's murder. Well, he could keep the truth. Tommy Kane was interested only in securing his freedom – as far away from Rico as he could get, with Ellie at his side. It was a risk going back into town to collect her, but it was a risk he was prepared to take. With Dolan and his posse roaming the countryside, there would be few people in Rico looking for an escaped prisoner.

Tommy dug his heels into a horse reluctant to gallop in the early afternoon heat. But it was Tommy who won the battle of wills and the horse gathered pace as the pair mounted a rise and headed back towards the town.

It was an hour into his ride for freedom that Tommy spotted them . . . a small group of four, maybe five, men barely 200 yards below him in the valley. Could they be Dolan and some of his posse?

Tommy reined in his grateful horse and dismounted. The men were heading in his direction. Searching frantically for a place where he could stay out of sight until the group passed, he spotted a break in the rocks that offered the chance of a hiding place.

Hurriedly, his actions bordering on panic, he dragged his horse through the narrow gap and into the cover of bushes beyond.. He waited, his Colt at the ready. If they were Dolan's men he would go down fighting and not at the end of a rope.

The minutes passed. The men were clearly in no hurry and Tommy knew it was not only the afternoon heat that was causing the rivers of sweat to run down his neck and back. He was scared.

The sound of slow moving hoofs came closer and Tommy held his breath. Absurdly, he just hoped that his horse could do the same. Then there were voices . . . raised in anger. The riders stopped barely a dozen yards from Tommy's hiding hole. Then, in a loud voice he clearly recognized, came the order, 'I've told you, Munroe, right now you work for us. What you do when you're finished here is your business. Until then, you take orders like the rest of us! We do it his way.'

Tommy strained to catch a look at the men. Who the hell was Zeb Maddox ordering about? And why? The face of the man flashed briefly into view. He was a thin-faced figure with a crooked smile that did not leave his lips even in his anger.

'So the sooner we get done the sooner I can go after McCabe. And this time I'll make sure he won't be around to tell the story.'

Then, another voice – another Tommy recognized – a cowhand who had also given evidence against him at the trial.

'Seems to me you had your chance, Jay, and you oughta forget McCabe,' he said sneeringly.

'Hell'll freeze before I ask for your advice, Moose,' Munroe snapped back. 'I owe McCabe and he's gonna get what's coming.'

Maddox interrupted. 'Like I said, we've got business, Munroe – till that's done you work for the man. Now, come on, let's get moving.'

There was a sudden rush of activity out of Tommy's line of sight and he listened while the men rode off down the trail, waiting for the silence before he could relax.

Mopping his brow, he crept cautiously out of his hiding place and watched as the cloud of dust disappeared into the distance. Pulling his horse back on to the track, he mounted up. Things had changed. A chance encounter with Maddox and a man called Munroe altered everything. He could not ride off and leave Ben to become a sitting target just as he had been six years before. Ellie Jacobs, a return to Wyoming and a peaceful life on the family farm would have to wait.

Tommy Kane had a duty to warn his rescuer that his life was in danger not only from a posse but also from another man swearing to kill him.

SIX

Ben McCabe followed Mollie up the steps and into the small house of the Cooper ranch. Coral, the housekeeper, fussed at the rare sight of a stranger in the ranch house – especially a man, since Miss Mollie had rarely 'entertained' these past three years.

'Don't fret, Coral,' Millie smiled. 'Mr McCabe isn't going to bite. Just bring us some coffee.'

The woman scuttled out of the room and Ben walked to the rear of the house. Beyond the corral, the land stetched away towards a pine forest and even further a range of mountains.

'This all yours?' Ben asked.

Mollie chuckled. 'Less than a quarter of what you see belongs to us Coopers. The rest is DX land. 'Cept the mountains, of course, I reckon God owns those.'

'You said us Coopers? There's more than you then?'

Mollie perched herself on the corner of a desk. 'Force of habit, I guess. My father died in a stage accident a couple of years back and my brother Jed ran off to dig for gold – or steal it if that turned out to be easier. That left

67

me and a few cowhands to look after the place.'

'Why didn't you sell up and leave?'

'Don't know, really. Except that the only offer came from Jake Dexter and it was less than half what it was worth. Besides. . . .' She fell silent.

Ben waited for her to continue.

'The Coopers and the Dexters have never got along so I reckoned Pa would not have wanted me to sell out to them. So here I am – with no place to go, a few hundred head of beef and four cowhands and a maid to support.'

Ben suspected she wasn't telling him the whole truth, but he let it pass. So far none of it was any of his business although the more he studied the woman the more he felt inclined to help things along. Mollie Cooper was indeed a captivating lady.

'No husband?'

Mollie rose from her perch on the desk and walked across the room. 'No,' she said simply, and stepped outside on to the veranda.

Ben was about to follow her when Coral re-entered the room with a tray of china coffee cups.

She turned to leave when Ben called her back.

'Tell me, it's none of my business, Coral, but what's eating your mistress?

The maid looked this new visitor over. He had a kindly sort of face, not the usual rough and ready cowpokes who normally called in looking for work. Glancing anxiously towards Mollie who was out on the veranda, she said quickly, 'It's not my place to say, mister but if you need to know then ask her about Buck Dexter. That's all ah'm sayin'.'

Ben filled two of the cups and carried them out to where Mollie was staring towards the distant mountain range. She didn't turn as he handed her a cup and for a moment she said nothing other than a polite thanks.

Eventually Ben broke the silence.

'You should sell up and leave, Mollie. There's nothing here for a woman like you.'

She spun round and glared at him angrily. Then, without another word, she softened and went back into the house. He followed and waited as she went across to her large oak desk and opened a drawer. She removed a small bundle of papers and tossed them in his direction.

'You said you wanted to help,' she said quietly. 'Then I suggest you read that and tell me you still think the same.'

With that, she stormed out of the room.

Ben settled into a seat behind the desk and spread the papers in front of him. On top of the pile was a Wanted poster, the kind that had once carried his own name and face with a reward of $2,000.

The face staring back at him bore a vague resemblance to Mollie Cooper. It did not need much imagination to assume that Mollie and the wanted man were related.

The name confirmed it: Jed Cooper – Wanted for Murder and Robbery.

The next sheet of paper was a copy of a newspaper that bore the headline: BANK RAIDERS MURDER TELLER. POSSE HUNT COOPER GANG. Ben read through the newspaper report on the bank raid in Colorado followed by a shoot-out in which one of the bank robbers was wounded in the leg making a getaway.

The newspaper also linked the raid to a stage hold-up

by the same gang and Jed Cooper had been recognized as its leader.

After escaping from the bank raid, Jed had gone into hiding, but what the *Southern Colorado Clarion* did not report – because nobody knew – was that Jed headed home to the security of the isolated family ranch.

Ben studied several other papers all connected with the exploits of outlaw Jed Cooper. Folding the sheets into a neat pile he rose from his chair and rejoined Mollie on the veranda.

'What happened?'

Mollie continued to stare into the distance.

'Buck Dexter and me, we were walking out together at that time. We were even trying to find a way to tell our folks that we were planning to get married and they could carry on their stupid feud without us.

'But then Jed turned up nursing a leg wound. He looked like a man on the run and he told me what happened. Jed didn't amount to much, but he was my brother so I cared for him the best way I could.

'He had been home only a week when the law came and dragged him off. It was only a while later that I discovered how the marshals came to know where to find him.'

'The Dexters?' Ben suggested.

Mollie nodded. 'Not just the Dexters. Buck. It was Buck, the man I was planning to marry who told the law where to find my brother.'

'What happened to Jed?' Ben asked.

Mollie eventually turned to face him. There were tears in her eyes.

'He never made it to the fair trial that Buck and the marshals had promised. Shot while trying to escape, we were told.'

'And you and Buck?'

She wiped away the threat of tears. 'Buck isn't like the rest of the Dexters. He's a good man and he thought he had a duty to tell the law that Jed was hiding out at the ranch. I don't know, maybe part of me agreed with him, but I couldn't marry a man who had sent my brother to his death. We haven't spoken a civil word to each other since that day two years ago. And it's another reason I won't sell up and leave this place to the Dexter family.'

Mollie fell into another of her long silences and Ben sensed that she was through talking. They stood side by side gazing out at the impressive vista that was east Arizona. Ben's thoughts returned to his own plight – a man on the run for helping a convicted killer to escape the hangman's noose.

Now that Tommy had gone he was all alone, the prey in a manhunt of his own making.

Suddenly, he felt Mollie's hand on his arm.

'Looks like we're about to have company,' she said, pointing to a small cloud of dust emerging from the area of the forest at the foot of the mountain range. 'Six, maybe seven riders by the look of it,' she added. Ben followed the direction of the pointing finger. The cloud was approaching fast. These were clearly men in a hurry and McCabe needed no second guesses about the identity of the horsemen.

'Looks like it's time I wasn't here, Mollie,' he said. 'That'll be Sheriff Dolan and his posse and I'm one of the men he's looking for.'

Mollie's grip on his arm tightened.

'Frank Dolan? What's he wanting you for?'

'It's a long story, Mollie – best you don't know.' He shrugged himself free. 'I reckon it's time I was moving on.'

To Ben's surprise, Mollie laughed.

'Frank Dolan is Jake Dexter's man so if he's chasing you, I reckon you can't be all bad. I think you should find some place to hide – upstairs maybe – while I get rid of him and his lynch mob. Then you can tell me what this is all about.'

For the second time that day Tommy Kane found himself a hiding place to watch a group of riders. Only this time there was no mistaking their identity.

He had ridden at full gallop back to the creek where he had left Ben McCabe in a deep sleep only to find that the man who had staged his jail break had gone. But to where? Tommy rode east, scouring the countryside in search of his missing friend. He was about to give up when he spotted a small ranch house in the distance and heading in its direction was Sheriff Frank Dolan and his posse.

Tommy dismounted and watched as the sheriff and his men approached the house. A woman stood alone on the veranda and from what he could make out at the distance, she stepped down to meet the riders. He watched as the sheriff and the woman had a brief conversation that ended when the lawman swung his horse away and his men followed, heading off to the south slowly disappearing into the distance.

He was about to remount and resume his half-abandoned escape when the woman was joined on the balcony by a man in a bright red shirt and black vest and pants – he had found Ben McCabe.

'You're sure that's what you heard?'

Ben and Tommy Kane were sitting on the front porch of the Cooper ranch house.

Mollie had left them alone to talk things over after McCabe had explained that he and the new arrival had a problem that needed fixing. Her brief talk with Sheriff Dolan had left her in no need of two guesses to know what that problem was.

'Like I said, Ben, that's the name I heard – Jay Munroe.' He watched for some reaction but McCabe appeared to be deep in thought and stared straight ahead of him.

Tommy's patience was wearing thin. 'Look, I could've ridden away and forgotten all about this and I was sure as hell close to doing that. I didn't need to come back to find you – to warn you. If I hadn't spotted this place and seen Dolan and his mob riding off I might have done that.'

McCabe stayed silent. He had already listened to Tommy's explanation of why he had sneaked off and how he had planned to go back to Rico, collect Ellie and return to his family farm in Wyoming. And he conceded that fear had spurred young Tommy into that action and he could hardly blame him for that. The choice between a loving wife and life on a small family farm and the threat of a hangman's noose was no contest at all.

Exasperated, Tommy stood up and demanded, 'So, what you gonna do?'

McCabe had already thought about that. As soon as

Tommy had given him the news that Munroe was still hell bent on finishing the job he had started years earlier there could be only one course of action.

A showdown. He had to get to Munroe before Munroe got to him. And if that meant stepping on the toes of the Dexters, then that was the way it would have to be.

He rose from the bench and put his arm around the younger man.

'Thanks for coming back, Tommy. I'll watch my back from here on in.'

'But – what about me? You want me to stay?'

McCabe chuckled. 'Less than an hour ago you saw Dolan and his men head off south looking for us. Which means that there'll be nobody in Rico looking for a young kid. I reckon you should get yourself back there and start trying to persuade that young lady of yours that Wyoming's quite a pretty place to bring up a family.'

SEVEN

Alec Dexter was in a good mood. His saddle-bags were crammed with cash and gold and trinkets from the latest stage robbery. It had been a good day's trade: 10 maybe $15,000 for a few worn out rifles and a couple of cases of rotgut whiskey.

His agreement with the handful of renegades had brought him rich rewards from the day he had formed the alliance and planned the first of the raids. It was a partnership that suited everybody – the Apaches had no use for dollars and Alec could supply what they did want, guns and booze.

He could have gone along with the rest of them and settled for some small-time rustling and horse-thieving, but that would have left him in Buck's shadow. Buck was the brother who would get the ranch when the old man died. And that would be soon enough if the medical report Alec had found in the house safe was accurate. A tumour in the stomach, the specialist in Phoenix had confirmed. Alec felt a sense of importance with that knowledge. He doubted if Buck or their stepmother even knew that the old man had been to see a specialist. Sure, Buck would become the head of the biggest ranch in the area and own half the town of Rico, but he didn't know that their father was dying.

And if it wasn't Buck who was getting in his hair it was young Dave.

Pa's other little hero. Well, Dave was gone now and they had that kid locked up for the killing. That was another reason Alec was in a good mood.

Dave had never been a true Dexter as far as Alec was concerned. They had the same father and they lived in the same house, but they were never really brothers – just because the old man and Buck wanted it couldn't change the way he felt.

Alec was his own man and, thanks to the Indians, he was rich. It was time to move on, to leave Buck and the old man to their cows and their small-town politics.

But first there was one more thing he had to do. Dave and that kid Kane had tried it with old Doc Jacobs daughter. Now it was his turn. She wouldn't turn him down – or she'd be sorry.

It was sundown when McCabe and Mollie stood side by side and watched lovesick fugitive Tommy Kane ride off in the direction of Rico. Between them they had agreed that darkness would be the best cover if he wanted to get in and out of town unseen.

As they turned to move back into the house, Ben took the woman's arm.

'I asked you today if there was anything I could do to help you – now it looks as though I owe you. Why didn't you tell Dolan about me?'

Mollie smiled and shrugged.

'Maybe I just thought you'd got an honest face,' she said.

'And what about now?'

'You told me that Tommy didn't kill young Dave Dexter. He looked like a nice kid and I know Ellie Jacobs. She's a good judge so, well, I guess there are times when you just have to trust folk.' She paused before adding, 'And I sure as hell don't trust Frank Dolan as far as I can spit.'

Ben laughed. 'Thanks.'

They went inside the house and Mollie said, 'So that's young Tommy and his future taken care of – what about you? What are your plans?'

McCabe thought for a moment. 'As far as the law's concerned – even the law that isn't owned by the Dexters or run by Dolan – Tommy's on the run for murder. It may stop men like Frank Dolan chasing after him once he's outside the territory, but it won't stop the bounty hunters. Soon enough there'll be posters out offering a reward for Tommy Kane, wanted dead or alive. The Dexters and the town will put up the reward money. A thousand dollars, maybe more. Even Wyoming won't be far enough to be safe. Some gun-happy get-rich-quick gunslinger will hunt him down, and it will be all legal like. I know what that's like.

'Tommy and his family once saved my life and it's time I repaid the debt by finding out who really killed young Dave.'

When he fell silent Mollie suspected there was something else on his mind and he eventually continued,

77

'There are two other reasons for me to stay around. One – a man called Jay Munroe. He was the one who put a couple of bullets in me and thought he had done enough to kill me and collect a two thousand dollar reward. Now Tommy tells me he's riding with the DX ranch and he's anxious to finish the job.'

'And the second reason?'

'You.'

Ben pulled her to him and their lips met in a passionate kiss. Then, without another word, they linked arms and climbed the staircase to the bedroom which Mollie Cooper had once shared with Buck Dexter.

Tommy Kane rode as though his horse's tail was on fire, praying that even in the gathering darkness his mount would avoid all the pits and ruts of a well-used trail to Rico.

His thoughts also raced. Would Ellie agree to leave with him; or would Doc Jacobs stand in their way? Maybe even turn him in to Dolan? Moonrise helped to make the gallop easier and when he eventually reached the outskirts of town he gave his horse a grateful slap of thanks. He had made it so far – now for the difficult task of persuading Ellie to come with him.

Taking the back street behind the newspaper office, general store and barber's shop, Tommy felt his nerves on edge. Twice he spotted faces he knew but neither of the two men was sober enough to recognize the man walking his horse towards the doc's house. It was only when he emerged from the darkness of the back alley that Tommy froze. The Jacobs had a visitor.

A horse was tethered at the picket fence around the

house garden. A pinto. Tommy knew only one man around Rico who rode a pinto: Alec Dexter. But why would he be visiting Doc Jacobs? Had he learned that Tommy had escaped from jail and was here to ask Ellie and her father about him? He knew Tommy was sweet on Ellie. He may even have known that they were planning to marry. It was obvious he would reckon that she would know something of the whereabouts of the man she was courting.

Tommy hitched his horse to a post outside the stable yard and made his way cautiously towards the house. A light shone from the front room and he could make out raised voices. Slowly and taking care not to be heard, he crept across the neat flowerbed and lawn and crouched beneath the window.

The first voice he heard was the one he longed to hear for the rest of his life: Ellie. And she was angry.

'God forgive me, Alec Dexter, but I wouldn't marry you if you were the last man in Arizona. Now get out of my house before my father comes back and throws you out.'

There was a laugh – a chuckle of sarcasm.

'The doc? Throw me out? Come on, Ellie, that ain't gonna happen. You and me – we could make it together. I'm a rich man, more than you could hope to see – more than that Kane kid could ever give you. Especially now he's gonna hang for killing Dave.'

'I told you, Alec – get out of this house. You . . . you. . . .'

There was a silence before Tommy heard Alec's protest.

'I know you don't mean that, Ellie, a pretty girl like you. There's nobody here to see, why don't you and me—?'

Tommy heard the smack of a hand on flesh followed by a foul curse and another smack, then a scream.

'Listen. bitch. That pretty face of yours ain't gonna look so nice tomorrow if—'

Tommy had heard more than enough. Springing to his feet, he raced to the front door of the house and, raising his boot, kicked it open. He burst in to see Alec Dexter tearing at Ellie's dress and the girl he loved scratching at her assailant's face.

Without a second thought, Tommy launched himself at Alec, gripping him around the throat and dragging him backwards.

Ellie scrambled away and edged out of reach. Tommy swung the other man around and although Dexter was much stronger, the rage inside him spurred Tommy on. Lashing out wildly, he connected flush on Alec's jaw and sent him crashing into an armchair. He had no chance to regain his feet before Tommy followed up his attack diving for the throat.

The chair splintered under their combined weight and Ellie screamed as the two men rolled across the floor. Tommy was the first to his feet and it was only then that Alec recognized his attacker.

'You bastard, Kane!' he snapped, reaching for his gun. 'I'll save the hangman a job.'

But he was too slow. His hand had hardly touched the six-shooter before Tommy's boot smashed into his wrist and sent the weapon spinning across the room.

Alec squealed in pain, but Tommy was far from finished. The fury inside him had reached fever pitch. Gripping Alec by the throat, he pulled him to his feet only to send him crashing back to the floor with a vicious forearm smash that broke Alec's nose and sent blood spurting across his face.

Tommy followed it up with a wild kick to the groin. He was oblivious to Ellie's screaming at him to stop.

'On your feet, you yeller coward, Dexter.'

Tommy was blind to anything other than the man lying groaning at his feet – so blind that he didn't see Alec reach for the discarded gun until it was almost too late. Dexter was about to squeeze the trigger when Tommy drew his own Colt and fired. Alec Dexter screamed as the bullet ripped into his arm.

He rolled away and sagged to the floor. Tommy raised his gun and prepared to put another bullet in the man who had been trying to rape his wife-to-be.

But Ellie's scream stopped him. She raced towards him and threw her arms around his neck. They stood together as Alec rolled about in agony as the pain took hold. Frozen, the young couple were still staring at the stricken man when Doc Jacobs walked into the room.

'In the name of God! What's happened?' the doctor gasped, at the sight of Tommy Kane, gun in hand, and his daughter staring down at the stricken figure on the floor.

'He's shot me! The bastard's shot me!' Alec screamed. 'Help me, Doc.' Noah Jacobs stayed calm. Tommy and Ellie stood silently by while Alec clutched his arm and writhed in pain.

'Doc,' he pleaded again, 'I'm hurtin' real bad.'

Jacobs hurried across the room and knelt beside the wounded man. He examined the gunshot wound and then turned to his daughter and the man clinging to her.

It was only then that he noticed Ellie's torn dress and shattered look. He looked directly at Tommy and there was a look of contempt on his face.

'I don't know what's gone on here but I want you out of here. You've already been convicted of murdering one Dexter and now you've wounded another. I want you out of here and out of my daughter's life for good or so help me, I'll—'

'Doc! Please!' Alec yelled.

'Don't worry, son, you'll live. I'll get you patched up and take you out to the ranch.'

Ellie rushed forward. 'Pa, you don't understand. This isn't Tommy's fault. He was only trying to protect me.'

Noah Jacobs rose to his feet and gripped his daughter's arms.

'That man is trouble, Ellie. He's been nothing but trouble since you got to know him. I can't let you—' He didn't finish. The slamming of the door caused him to spin round. A sigh or relief escaped his lungs as he saw that he had got his wish. Tommy Kane had gone.

There was a sombre silence around the supper table at the DX ranch. Jake Dexter had suffered a bad day of increasing pain and he knew that the time had come to tell his wife and sons that his days were numbered; that his life was ebbing away.

The news hit them hard. Elizabeth had spent the early evening alone in her room and when she emerged for her evening meal her eyes betrayed the fact that she had spent several hours crying. Buck had urged his father that more could be done, that there were specialist hospitals back East where doctors could help him.

Eventually the old man had convinced his son that

everything that could be done had been done and there was nothing anybody – not even the big city doctors – could do to delay his death.

The three of them sat around the table, their meals untouched, and gazed hopelessly into empty space before Buck finally broke the strained silence.

'Alec's missing again – we don't get much out of him these days,' he said pointing at the empty chair.

The old man was grateful for any conversation but he was quick to defend the younger brother.

'Don't be too hard on him, Buck, I reckon Alec's not cut out for ranch work.'

The eldest son grunted. He had long since worked that out, but he had never managed to learn what exactly Alec did around the place. Even the foreman Joe Kelly never seemed quite sure what he was up to much of the time.

The conversation turned to the spate of rustling that had plagued the DX and neighbouring ranches over recent weeks and the fact that Sheriff Dolan was failing miserably in his search for the culprits.

'I wouldn't trust Frank Dolan to clear out a barn,' Buck said sourly. 'The people of Rico deserve a lot better than him for a sheriff.'

'Maybe,' the old man muttered.

Suddenly, Elizabeth rose from the table and rushed from the room in a flood of tears. Her husband was dying, a slow, painful death and here he was with his eldest son chatting casually about the competence of a town sheriff.

'Leave her,' Dexter said quietly, as Buck rose to follow her from the room. 'It's hard for her to take, son, and she's going to need you when. . . .' His voice died away but

Buck got the message.

It was getting close to midnight when a sudden disturbance outside was followed by a banging on the door and a voice, urgent, demanding, 'Mr Dexter! Buck! It's Joe Kelly! You better come.'

The old man struggled to his feet, but Buck was first to the door. He pulled it open to find a flustered foreman on the doorstep. Clinging on to him, his arm wrapped in a sling and a bloodstained bandage hiding much of his face, was Alec. Doc Jacobs was sitting in a rig at the bottom of the porch steps.

Jake Dexter gasped in horror at the sight of his son in such a state.

But he quickly regained his self-control.

'Who did this?' he demanded.

Alec groaned a curse. Kelly and Buck helped the injured man into the house but the old man wanted to know more. Striding down the steps he confronted Doc Jacobs.

'You gonna tell me, Noah?'

The two men had known each other for many years – they had even been friends in their youth – but the medical man had allowed the friendship to cool when Jake Dexter and his sons began to act as though they owned not only the businesses in the town of Rico but also its people. But he could see that his former friend was in no state or mood for confrontation.

'I can only tell you what I saw – and what my daughter told me,' he said, 'though Alec may have another story.'

'Tell me,' Dexter barked impatiently. 'Who did this to my son?'

Reluctantly, Noah Jacobs explained what he had seen.

'Alec had already been shot when I got home. He was lying there and my daughter's dress had been torn—'

'Who, Noah? Who did this?'

Sighing, Jacobs leaned forward. 'It was Tommy Kane. He shot Alec, but my girl said he was only defending her.'

Jake Dexter turned away and mounted the steps to go inside.

As he reached the door he turned to face the doctor.

'Next time you see Tommy Kane tell him from me. He's already taken one son from me and I'll be coming for him. He's going to pay, Noah, and I don't give a damn about your daughter's feelings.'

EIGHT

The following morning the DX ranch had another visitor. Mollie Cooper called.

'I need to talk to Buck,' she said, when Joe Kelly met her with something less than a warm welcome. Mollie had spurned Kelly's advances over the years and he was not the sort of man to take rejection with a friendly smile or a shrug.

'Maybe he ain't here, Mollie,' he said coldly, as she dismounted outside the ranch house. 'An' I don't think the family's takin' any visitors right now. Not after what happened to Alec.'

'What could happen to Alec that wouldn't improve the whole of Arizona?' she said with heavy sarcasm.

'Well, since you ain't heard, Alec got himself shot up last night by that kid who already killed Dave. Right now, Buck and some of the boys are out hunting the crazy killer down. And this time there won't be no trial.'

Mollie detested Kelly but there was no reason to disbelieve him. This meant that a posse led by Frank Dolan and a bunch of ranch hands hell bent on their own brand of bloody justice were on Tommy's trail. The kid didn't have a chance.

Yet she believed the man who had spent the night in her bed had told her the truth: Tommy Kane was not the man who killed Dave Dexter.

'Maybe I should talk to the old man,' she said after a brief thought.

'Sorry, Mollie – I've got my orders. No visitors.'

'Listen, Joe, you may not be my favourite cowhand in the territory, but I'm here on business. Why don't you just go in there and tell your boss I'm here. Then maybe – just maybe – you'll get to keep your job as foreman here.'

Kelly scowled. If he sent her away and she really did have business with the DX, old Dexter would be furious; if he let her in. . . .

'Right, Mollie,' he said at last. 'Can I tell the old man what your business is about?'

She smiled. 'Sure you can, Joe. Tell him I'm thinking of selling up and moving on and I'm giving him the first chance to buy me out.'

It was a lie, but it suited her purpose. The Dexters had always been interested in the Cooper place and for her part, she wanted to arrange a meeting between Buck and McCabe. Ben had told her of his earlier meeting with the eldest Dexter son and how he appeared to have some sympathy with the idea that somebody other than Tommy might have killed Dave. Ben knew that it was a long shot but if he could get Buck alone, away from the surroundings of the DX, he might have more chance of persuading him to help. From his own experience, McCabe knew that the so-called witnesses to the killing were hardly dependable. A bogus offer of sales talk seemed to be the best way of contriving such a get-together.

'Wait here,' Kelly said sourly and went into the house, emerging a few minutes later to usher Mollie inside.

Jake Dexter was standing beside his desk and Mollie was shocked at the sight of the man who had once been her father's friend. She had not seen the owner of the DX for more than a year and she was staggered by the change in him.

Gone were the full, florid features, the barrel chest and upright figure of the man who had once tried to bully her into a sale. This was a shadow of the Jake Dexter she had known. He was pale-faced, had shed several pounds and he stooped.

He tried to smile but it did not come easily even though the old man truly liked Mollie Cooper.

When she had been walking out with his eldest son he had had high hopes that the DX and Cooper brands would unite for no better reason than the marriage of the two young lovers.

But it was not to be. The courtship ended and with it went Dexter's hopes of expanding his already huge empire even further.

There had been a time when he and Mollie's father, Clayton Cooper, shared a dream of turning the small town of Rico into one of Arizona's leading cattle and commercial centres.

And, despite their regular differences over land and watering rights, they had a mutual respect that developed into friendship.

All that ended when Dexter backed Frank Dolan for

sheriff. Clayton Cooper knew Dolan for what he was – a gun for hire to the highest bidder. And that bidder happened to be the Dexters.

But Clayton Cooper was dead and now his daughter was in the house eager to talk about the sale of her ranch.

'Good to see you, Mollie,' he said and meant it. 'Kelly tells me you want to talk about selling your place and moving on.'

'I think the time's right, Jake, and if I can get the right price.'

'Your daddy taught you well,' Dexter said with a weak smile. Suddenly he leaned forward and gripped the back of a chair. There was pain in his face and Mollie rushed forward to offer him support but he recovered quickly and forced another smile.

'I'm fine, Mollie.' He steadied himself and, although she was not sure that he was as fine as he pretended to be, she let it pass.

'I'm told Buck's running things for you now,' she ventured. 'Maybe he could come over – we could talk about it.'

'I'd like that, Mollie. I was sorry when you and Buck . . . well, went your separate ways.'

Mollie knew that his concern was real enough.

It was Jake Dexter who had encouraged his eldest son 'to go courting that pretty neighbour, Mollie Cooper'. And even if the original intention was to get his hands on the Cooper spread to add to the expanding DX, Buck had been a kind and considerate suitor.

They agreed to set up a meeting as soon as Buck returned and Mollie was about to leave when the old man suddenly asked, 'Why the change of heart, Mollie? It's not so long ago you wouldn't sell the Cooper place to us Dexters before hell froze over.'

She laughed. That was true enough.

'Things change, Jake,' she said simply.

Again, she turned to leave only to be stopped by another question.

'You heard about Alec?' Dexter asked.

'I did. Joe Kelly told me. How is he?' She wasn't really interested in any good news about Alec Dexter.

'He'll recover,' the old man told her, 'and it's why Buck's not here, right now. He's out hunting down that young killer Tommy Kane and his sidekick – the man who got him out of jail.'

Mollie waited for him to go on.

'A man called McCabe. Ex-lawman who turned bad,' he said.

'We all know at least one of those, Jake,' Mollie said with a wry smile. 'The name's Frank Dolan.'

Dexter managed a friendly chuckle. 'Dolan does as I tell him, Mollie, but this man McCabe – I've been hearing things about him.'

Mollie's expression gave nothing away even though she was eager to hear more. The old man did not let her down.

'McCabe was a lawman up in Kansas before joining the railroad as a security man. They say he got away with twenty thousand dollars and killed a harmless old man. He's been on the run ever since.'

Mollie thought about what she was hearing.

How much of it was true? Was Ben McCabe – the man

who had shared her bed the previous night – an outlaw? She was reluctant to believe that a man who showed such tender touch and consideration could be a cold-blooded killer and a thief.

'Why are you telling me this, Jake?' she asked, suddenly aware that the old man might even suspect something. But her worst fears were soon quelled.

'You're all alone in that house out there and there's every chance these two will still be around these parts. I just worry for you, Mollie. You need a man around.'

Mollie chuckled. 'You matchmaking again, Jake? I'll be fine. I can take care of myself. I've been doing just that ever since. . . .' She meant to say it was ever since her father's death but she let it slide. 'Tell Buck I'll see him tomorrow and I'm sorry about Alec. Hope he's fixed up soon.'

She left the DX ranch still wondering about Ben McCabe and hoping he was the man she thought and not the killer on the run.

McCabe listened without interruption to Mollie's report of her visit to the DX and her meeting with Jake Dexter. Another meeting – this time with Buck – had been arranged; the old man was prepared to talk about a sale that Mollie had no intentions of carrying out.

And Ben McCabe had been branded a lawman turned bad.

As she finished relating the details, Ben knew it was his turn to speak.

'Some of what he told you is true,' he said at last, studying Mollie's face for some reaction.

'How much is some?' she asked.

McCabe thought about that. How much was the truth? A lawman turned bad and on the run? He wouldn't be the first. Who in his right mind would take on a job where at any moment he could stop a bullet from some trigger-happy kid who wanted to show that he was the fastest gun in the territory? Or worse, a bullet in the back from somebody he had locked up some time in the distant past? Or just a town drunk? And all for less than fifty dollars a month?

Eventually he broke the silence.

'I was a town lawman once,' he said, 'and I guess if Jake Dexter has been listening to certain people, they'd tell him I'd gone bad.'

Mollie sat silently and waited for more.

'Six years ago,' Ben continued, wishing there was a glass of whiskey near at hand, 'Tommy Kane and his younger brother Josh saved my life. I was shot and left for dead in a creek near their family's farm in Wyoming.

'Their grandfather pulled a bullet out of my chest and another had grazed my head.' Out of habit, his hand moved towards the fading scar on his temple.

'The boys' mother nursed me back to health, but when I came round, I could not remember anything – not even my name. All I had was a Wanted poster with my face on it and carrying the offer of a two thousand dollar reward.'

He paused but Mollie did not interrrupt.

'I was still at the Kane place when two men came gunning for me, one of them was an ex-lawman called Ned Miller, and his young sidekick, name of Frank Beckman. They were after the reward, but I vaguely remembered Miller from somewhere. There was a shoot-out and Miller ended up dead.

'Gradually my memory returned in bits and pieces and in time remembered I had been his deputy up in Kansas before I joined the railroad. But I struggled to find a way back to where I had been before I was left lying in that creek.

'I had been set up by a man called Mitchell Dredge. He was the depot manager of the railroad at Charlsburg where I was the company's security officer. I was out of town on family business when Dredge staged the robbery, killed the old man and sent out the Wanted bills with my name on. Dredge was cunning. He made the folk believe that the railroad had put up the reward and he even used another bill bearing the name of Jeff Banner which was a name I had used while on confidential railroad business.'

Mollie's curiosity eventually got the better of her.

'Then what happened?'

Encouraged that she was at least halfway to believing his story, Ben continued. 'Dredge sent three men after me – Miller, the kid, and another mean piece of poison named Jay Munroe.

'Like I said, I shot Miller and eventually tracked down Dredge. But I was too late. Munroe and he had finally reached an end to their partnership. Jay gunned him down and took all the money that had been emptied from the railroad safe – and anything else Dredge had stashed away.'

Mollie smiled. 'Sounds familiar – thieves falling out over loot.'

Ben nodded. 'But there was more to it than that. A

woman named Carla Blake was knifed in an alley the night Munroe ran out of town.'

'Did you find him?'

'Oh, I got him all right. And what was left of the money. I dragged him back to Charlsburg to stand trial for robbery and murder.'

'Then?'

Ben shrugged. 'Then? I can't tell you. I left Munroe locked up in the jail of Sheriff Brad Nicholls to wait for the circuit judge. I didn't hang around to find out the verdict.'

'Why not? Since you pulled him in, I'd have thought—'

Ben held up his hand to silence her.

'Two reasons, Mollie. Brad Nicholls was an honest sheriff. But he was married to Munroe's sister. And the family was rich. They hired the best lawyer in Cheyenne to come and defend Munroe. There were no witnesses to the killing and, as far as the railroad was concerned, it was Dredge who had set up the robbery. The chances were that Munroe would walk free – or at worst get a couple of years in the state prison. I didn't want to be around to see that.'

Mollie nodded, then said, 'You said there were two reasons. What was the other?'

'I returned the killer and the thief; I didn't return the stolen money.'

Mollie looked straight into McCabe's eyes.

'So – old Jake was right about that. You are on the run?'

Ben chuckled. 'Guess so, but after all this time I don't think there'll be too many lawman hunting for me – especially out here in Arizona.' He could see that the flippancy did not impress her so he decided that, as he had come this far, the whole truth should come out.

'Remember I said I was out of town on family business when the robbery took place?'

She looked away and did not reply.

Ben stood up and reached for the whiskey he needed.

'My sister had sent me a letter that tore me to pieces, Mollie. She was trapped in a marriage to a brute of a man who called himself a preacher. Tobias Troon was through and through evil. He beat my sister, kept her prisoner in her own home, robbed and swindled vulnerable widows. Mollie, I have killed a few men in my time – most, if not all of them, bad, but I've never enjoyed it – except the day I put a bullet in Tobias Troon and rid the world of a violent creature.'

He paused, almost gasping for breath and Mollie could see that the hate for Tobias Troon was still there even after all these years. Slowly, Ben drained his glass and refilled it from the decanter on the desk.

'What Troon did to my sister sent her into a hospital for the mentally ill back in Chicago. I used that railroad money to pay for her treatment.

'They owed me that much, by God they did!' he finished vehemently and emptied the glass for the second time.

He was visibly shaking as he returned to his chair and Mollie could see that here was a man who had been to Hell and was still only just coming back.

He sighed, tried to squeeze another drink out of the empty glass and said, 'So, there you have it, Mollie. One-time lawman, railroad thief and now, to cap it all, the man who broke a convicted killer out of Rico jail. Old man

Dexter wasn't far wrong, was he?'

Mollie walked over and put her arms around him, but he did not respond.

Instead he said simply, 'And I've not finished yet. I've got some more business that will lead to another killing. I may have put Jay Munroe behind bars, but I haven't finished with him yet. He was the man who put two bullets in me and left me for dead. I owe him.'

NINE

The bunkhouse at the DX ranch was in darkness and silent except for the heavy breathing and snoring of its occupants.

Outside, the two men who had crept stealthily from the room spoke in whispers. The taller man gave the orders, the other listened, nodding occasionally in agreement. Then, making their way across the yard, they led their horses from the corral and out into the night.

That fool Alec may have got himself shot up but Zeb and Moose had others to meet and there was work to be done before daybreak.

Buck Dexter arrived at the Cooper house later than expected and Mollie was on hand to rush out to meet him when he tied up his horse at the rail. Surprisingly, her heart seemed to skip a beat and she knew instantly why she had been charmed by the eldest of the Dexter sons.

Not yet in his late thirties, he was what Mollie imagined Jake to have been in his younger days – broad-shouldered and square-jawed handsome, not unlike the man who had recently come into her life.

Except there was no mystery about Buck Dexter. She had known him since childhood and although he lacked the toughness and coldness of his father, she knew he could be as hard as any of them.

He smiled as he approached and he was full of apologies.

'I'd have been here sooner but we've had more trouble in the night.'

'More rustlers?'

He nodded. 'Down at the south pasture. Not sure how much beef's gone this time, but Joe Kelly's got men down there now. They can't have gotten too far. Maybe this time we'll catch them and the steers.'

But she could tell from his tone that he was not optimistic. And with good reason. There were so many hidden canyons and ravines, perfect for keeping cattle under cover until the heat was off and the time was right to move them on.

The DX had suffered more than any other spread in the district but that was understandable – the DX was bigger than all the rest.

'Anyway, it's good to see you again, Mollie.'

'You too, Buck. Let's go inside. We can talk there, and there's somebody there I think you've already met.'

Puzzled, Buck followed her up the steps and into the house. It was as he remembered it – neat, clean, expensively furnished with fittings from back East, including the wide mahogany table and the plush armchairs where they had shared many an evening meal and a late-night drink.

There was just one major change – the man sitting at

the bureau. He got up and walked across the room to greet them as they entered the house.

It was Mollie who spoke.

'Buck, I think you've met Ben McCabe.'

Dexter glowered at the man who was now extending his hand in friendly greeting.

'You were round at the DX asking about that kid, Kane,' he said, ignoring the outstretched hand. 'Now he's gone missing. Somebody broke him out of Rico jail.'

'So I heard,' Ben said, 'and you think that might have been me?'

Buck Dexter eyed the stranger. He was maybe a couple of inches shorter than Buck himself, two or three years younger and maybe a few pounds lighter although he had the same dark, handsome features – Buck had never been coy about his good looks – and there was a similarity in their body shape.

'It figures – you're the only stranger in these parts to have asked about the kid. You even went to the jail to see him and talked Frank Dolan into letting you into the cell. Dolan's been to the DX – he reckons it was you who broke him out.'

There was a strained silence in the room before McCabe said, 'I can see things look bad for me, but I think if I'd freed the kid I'd be out of here and long gone.'

Buck frowned. 'Guess so. But what you doing here? Mollie and I have business to talk.'

'She told me, asked my advice as a family friend. I knew her father. Hey, don't worry. I know nothing about ranches. I'm just passing through. If you two want to talk business I'll be on my way.'

Mollie stepped between the two men.

'Don't be silly, Ben. Buck and I have plenty of time to talk business. You don't have to rush away.'

They small-talked for a few minutes before McCabe decided to make his opening gambit.

'Sorry to hear about your brother Alec getting shot. Mollie was telling me—'

Buck frowned and shot the woman a meaningful glance.

'Seems to me Mollie's been telling you a lot of things, McCabe,' he said. He shrugged. 'If you did help Kane break out of jail, you might like to know he put a bullet in Alec. Looks like he's trying to work his way through the Dexter family.' There was bitterness in his tone.

'Let me tell you, mister, we'll get him and this time he'll hang for sure.' Ben gave that threat some thought.

'When I visited you at the DX, I got the idea that maybe you thought Tommy hadn't killed Dave. Was I wrong about that?'

'You were wrong. Judge and jury decided that Kane killed young Dave and now he's put my other brother in a sling. Don't look this way for any support.'

'You saw it happen?' Ben asked.

'No – not the shooting. I just heard the commotion and Alec yelling from the alley. But there were others who saw it – the foreman Joe Kelly and a couple of the hands.'

He turned away and faced Mollie. 'Now, Mollie, can we talk business and in private?'

McCabe decided not to push it any further but he now knew that if Tommy Kane didn't shoot Dave Dexter – one of those did. But which one – and why?

He smiled at Buck.

'I'll let you and Mollie get on and talk over your business.' He turned to the woman. 'I'll be outside if you need me, Mollie, but somehow, I think Buck here will be offering you a good price. If you want my advice I'd take it.' He grinned and she made a face as he left.

Ben took a leisurely stroll around the yard at the back of the Cooper house while Mollie and Buck held their 'business' talks over a sale that would never take place. He needed the time to consider his next move. Four men – Joe Kelly, the two ranch hands and Alec Dexter – had witnessed the killing. All four had given evidence that Tommy Kane had shot Dave Dexter and Buck had added his own evidence – that he had chased and cornered Tommy and delivered him to the sheriff. It was more than enough to convince the jury that they had their killer.

But Ben was certain Tommy was not the gunman which meant that one of those five had shot young Dave Dexter. But the question still nagged away at him. Why?

He was still no closer to an answer when he was jolted out of his reverie by the sight of a rider approaching at full gallop. As he got closer Ben recognized him as the cowhand he had crossed on the road to the DX ranch – Zeb Maddox.

Hurriedly finding himself a hiding place in a nearby barn, he waited and watched as Maddox dismounted and raced up the steps to the house. Seconds later Buck and Maddox came out of the house, quickly mounted and galloped off into the distance. As their dustcloud disappeared over the rise Mollie came out of the house.

Ben left the secrecy of the barn and went across to join her.

'What happened?'

Mollie's expression was grim. 'Don't know for sure, but it had something to do with the old man. When I saw him yesterday he looked seriously ill. Buck didn't say much, except that he had to go – Jake had been taken bad.'

Ben could see that her concern was genuine but he made a feeble effort to lift her spirits.

'I reckon you haven't agreed to a sale?'

She smiled but only briefly.

'What do you think? Now, let's go inside and you can tell me all about what you are planning to do next.'

She took his arm and they went into the house. What Ben McCabe had in mind had nothing to do with clearing Tommy Kane, or finding the killer of Dave Dexter: it had much more to do with Mollie Cooper.

His voice was little more than a hoarse whisper and Buck had to lean close to hear the words coming from the parched lips of the man on the bed. They all knew – his wife, his eldest son and Jake Dexter himself – that the end was not far away. The old man could not count on seeing another sunrise.

'Where's Alec? Is he here?'

Buck Dexter cursed silently. The old man had already forgotten. Alec was upstairs in his room, nursing his gunshot wound and refusing to come down the stairs.

'He'll be here soon, Pa, you just get some rest now,' he said aloud.

The old man gripped his son's wrist but it was the feeble

grip of a man whose strength had deserted him.

'I need you to promise me, son. Take care of Alec – he's
. . . he's not bad really and if he is, blame me. It's how I
raised him. You're the strong one, Buck. Make him listen
to you.' He slumped back on to the pillow.

You raised us both the same, Buck thought, and he's
not here when you need him.

Elizabeth tried to comfort her husband, gently
mopping his brow. She looked pleadingly at her stepson,
searching his face for something to cling to. There was
nothing.

Buck rose from the bedside chair and walked out on to
the veranda. His father's death was only a matter of hours
away and after that the DX would be his. But how would
Alec react to the news? Buck allowed himself an ironic
smile. Stupid question. He knew exactly how Alec would
react – the same way he always did when he felt he was
being treated unfairly. He would lash out.

He turned and looked up at the window of his younger
brother's room. Then he went back inside to be with his
dying father.

TEN

Tommy Kane pulled the buggy to a halt and eyed the HOTEL board swaying in the gentle breeze. Darkness was approaching and they had travelled a long way; out of Arizona Territory and into Colorado. But the last few miles had been covered in a silence broken only occasionally by Ellie's worried questioning. Tommy had smiled back his reassurances but, in truth, no, everything was not fine. He was a troubled man with a heavy burden on his mind.

It was more than two days since they had left Rico following his wounding of Alec Dexter and he had left Ben McCabe to fight on his behalf.

He climbed down from the buggy and reached up to help Ellie. It was time for both of them to face up to what he had to do.

Dragging Ellie's carpet-bag from the back of the rig he led her up the two steps and into the hotel.

The clerk behind the desk, a man in his mid-fifties with a full head of grey hair and the paunch of somebody unused to daily exercise, greeted them with a friendly smile.

'Evenin' folks. You young'uns lookin' for a room?'

Tommy removed his hat. 'My fiancée would like your best room – I have to go out of town for a few days.'

Alarmed, Ellie gripped his arm.

The clerk had already turned to reach into the rack of keys behind the desk so he missed the exchange of looks between the young pair. Tommy scrawled an illegible signature in the register and took the key to Room 10 from the clerk, ignoring the man's enthusiastic description of the best room in the house overlooking the schoolhouse and the church and well out of sight of the town saloon. He led Ellie away from the desk and out of earshot of the hotel man.

'I'm really sorry, Ellie, but I gotta do this – I gotta go back.'

Ellie slumped on to a padded bench seat and tears welled up as she tried to focus on her young man's face.

'You can't leave me here,' she pleaded. 'We've come this far – nobody will be looking for you out here. We can be at your family farm in three or four days. We'll be safe there.'

Tommy slid on to the seat beside her and took her hand.

'We'll never be safe, Ellie, not while there are people who think I killed Dave. There'll be a price on my head – the Dexters will see to that – and bounty hunters don't ask questions.'

He paused, reached out and tried unsuccessfully to brush away her tears.

'Please, darling,' he begged, 'you have to understand. When we left your home in Rico I was desperate for us to get away – so desperate I didn't even think. I didn't care.'

She started to protest but he held his finger to her lips to silence her. 'You'll be fine here for two or three days – four at the most. I'll come back for you, as soon as this is over. I promise.'

'Over?' There was almost a sneer in her voice. 'This will never be over, Tommy. You're a wanted man and so is that . . . that hero of yours, Ben McCabe. I came with you because I love you and want to marry you and I was pre-pared to go to Wyoming, settle down and live on your farm – outside the law if that is what it took for us to be together. Now you tell me you're going back, maybe to put your head in a noose after all. And when you get to Rico, what will you tell my father about me? Will you tell him how you left me in a small backwater town in Colorado?'

They fell silent before Tommy eventually rose to his feet. She didn't understand that he could not leave Ben to fight a battle that wasn't even his. He had already tried to do that once.

'I'm begging you, Ellie. Ben McCabe's out there trying to track down the real killer and here am I hiding behind a woman's skirts. What does that make me?'

'Alive! That's what it makes you.' Ellie dabbed her eyes and got to her feet. She tried to put on a brave face.

'I see you've made up your mid, Tommy. So have I. I'll take a room here for tonight, maybe even tomorrow night as well. But if a stage or a train comes through this place heading in any direction that takes my fancy, I'll be on it. I won't wait around for news that somebody has put a bullet in your back. I can't do that – not even for you.'

She walked across to the desk, picked up her baggage

and headed up to the stairs to Room 10 where she would cry the whole night through.

As dusk was falling in the small Colorado town where Tommy Kane and Ellie Jacobs were making their sad farewells, the lights were going out for Jake Dexter.

At his bedside when he closed his eyes for the last time were his wife, his eldest son Buck and the DX foreman Joe Kelly.

Alec Dexter watched the touching scene of a dying father from the landing of the big house. As his step-mother slumped forward in a fit of tears that signalled the old man had breathed his last, Alec turned away and returned to his room. He had convinced himself that he felt nothing for the dying man and cared even less that the ranch was now in the hands of his brother.

The White Horse saloon was crammed with the usual assortment of gamblers, drinkers and off-key singers there for the piano playing and the dancing girls.

Jay Munroe was engrossed in his card game when the batwings burst open and a breathless Slim Ricketts, Rico's resident pedlar of the latest news and gossip, burst in.

Rushing to the bar, he grabbed an empty beer glass and slammed it down calling for order before announcing the information he reckoned would be worth a drink or two. But few of the saloon's customers paid him any attention until he yelled, 'Just heard! The old man's a goner! Jake Dexter died tonight.'

There was a stunned silence at the news – although Munroe allowed himself a twisted smile.

The old man would have left favourite son Buck in control of the DX and that would make Alec madder than a basket of rattlers and that was a situation he could exploit. Alec would listen to him – just like he had when they first met in that whorehouse in New Mexico.

Dexter had been drunk out of his mind and when the woman had tried to relieve him of more than he was willing to give, there had been a killing.

Sure, it may have been an accident, just like Alec said; that he had slapped her around and she had cracked her head in a bedside cabinet. Munroe had been in the next room and he had heard it all, so when he broke in and saw Alec Dexter standing over the lifeless body of a young girl, he took his chance.

Alec did not need too much persuading when Munroe suggested it would be a bad idea to have the Dexter name dragged into court, especially over a dead prostitute. Jay convinced him that the best thing to do was to put the girl into the bed – poor kid was no more than nineteen years old he thought as he carried her across the room – and hightail it out of town. By the time anybody noticed they would be back in Arizona. Alec crept down the back stairs and from that night the pair had been partners. And Jay Munroe learned everything he needed to know about the Dexters and the DX ranch.

He knew how Alec was consumed with jealousy about his young half-brother Dave and his older brother Buck. How he hated being the Dexter offspring who counted for nothing.

Alec needed little persuading to join Jay and the rest of them in their rustling operation. Not only would that help him get back at his father, it would also be a kick in the guts for Buck. And losing a few dozen head of beef would hardly bring ruin on the DX.

And then there was Alec's own piece of private enterprise – his agreement with those renegade Indians who would do his bidding for a keg of whiskey and a few rifles. And his bidding was a series of stage hold-ups. Sure, there was the odd killing, but Alec was careful not to get his hands dirty. There was always at least one survivor to report that Indians had attacked the stage just outside of town.

With Frank Dolan in the pay of the Dexters there was nothing to connect Alec with the robberies. Nothing except the cash and the gold that he had stored away in the deserted mineshaft that he thought nobody remembered.

Jay Munroe remembered, but he was keeping that information to himself until the right time came. Meanwhile, the death of Jake Dexter meant nothing more to Jay than another step into the DX inner circle. He threw his losing hand into the middle and watched the man across from him scoop up the notes and coins heaped on the table.

'Maybe this just ain't your night, Jay,' the man said, piling the coins neatly at his elbow and stuffing the notes into his shirt. 'Specially after what I just heard today.'

Munroe scowled.

'Yeah? And what'd you hear, Kal, that would be of any interest to me?' The man whose name was Kal grinned, exposing a row of tobacco-stained and decaying teeth, only partly hidden by an ungroomed moustache. Kal

Harper was one of the ranch hands at the DX and he had little affection for the man with the twisted grin. He scorned at the way Munroe had cultivated a friendship with Alec Dexter and spent precious little time out on the range with the rest of the hands.

'What I hear is that woman you been fancying's got herself a new feller just when you was thinking it was all clear since she ditched Buck.'

Jay leaned forward. Kal had got his attention. He had thought about Mollie Cooper for a long time, but while she was Buck's woman he had stayed clear. There were no prizes for crossing the Dexters over a woman.

He could see that Kal Harper was enjoying himself and although Jay had never been a man renowned for his patience – that failing had cost at least two people their lives – he decided to let the cowpoke have his moment.

'Don't know the feller myself,' Harper said eventually. 'Seems he ain't from these parts but Mollie – well, I hear she took to him straight off. . . .'

Jay grunted. 'An' has this stranger got a name, or is that something else you don't know.'

'Goes by the name of McCabe. Ben McCabe.'

The others at the table couldn't fail to notice the sudden change in Jay Munroe. That permanent crooked smile almost disappeared from his drawn features.

'Looks like you just heard the name of a ghost.'

It was a third member of the card-playing quartet – the town's undertaker Aristotle Beam – who spoke.

Jay Munroe tried to regain his composure.

'You could say that, old man,' he said at last. 'Yeah, I know him.'

110

He stopped short of telling the Rico mortician that he also planned to make the man his next customer. Jay remembered the day six years ago when he had gunned down McCabe, and left him for dead in a Wyoming creek.

Next time there would be no mistake.

ELEVEN

Tommy Kane mopped the sweat from his face and neck and patted his tired horse before dismounting. The long hard ride through the night and until the approaching twilight of the next day had brought him to the ridge over-looking the town where all his troubles had begun.

Now, as he stood and looked down over the rooftops of Rico his mind was in turmoil.

He was a young man torn between love and duty. Throughout the ride he had thought constantly of Ellie fretting away in a small hotel room in a strange town, waiting for his return. Desperately he searched his heart for reasons to persuade him that he was doing the right thing, that he could not leave Ben alone to fight his battles. It was his duty to give his support. But that sense of duty was weakening with every minute. Below him and less than a mile ahead was Rico, the town where they had built gallows specially to hang him for a murder he did not commit – the town that held the truth behind the shoot-ing of Dave Dexter.

It was a place to avoid and when he remounted, Tommy

steered his reluctant horse along the ridge, away from the roofs of houses and stores and the jailhouse that had once been his prison and headed out towards the trail that would eventually lead to the Cooper place and a reunion with Ben McCabe.

Frank Dolan's day had gone badly. His long search for the jailbreakers had produced nothing and he had decided that the posse were wasting time and the town's money so he had sent them home.

Now came the news that his benefactor and boss had died and the DX was in the hands of Buck Dexter. Buck was unlike his father; he would want his own lawman wearing the badge.

And to crown a bad day he had been taken for nearly a month's pay at the card table. He wondered how much longer he could wear the badge of sheriff of Rico. Perhaps it was time to move on, to claim his share of the money Alec and his buddies had made from their rustling. Maybe he might even push young Dexter for a few extra dollars to buy his silence over the little sideline he had with the Indians.

He chuckled over that. Alec Dexter was a fool if he seriously thought that nobody knew he was behind the stage robberies carried out by the renegades. Sure, it was a secret he had kept from the old man, but there was nothing going on around Rico that Frank Dolan did not know about.

That cheered him considerably and his mood had improved by the time he entered the office. The place was in darkness and he did not notice the figure standing against the far wall.

Lighting a table lamp, he was startled by a sudden movement and spun round to face his unexpected visitor.

'Hell! You almost frightened the life out of me there!' he said, suddenly relaxing. 'What you doing here at this time?'

The visitor smiled and it was only then that Dolan spotted the six-gun pointed straight at his chest.

'What—?'

He never got to finish the question. Two bullets ripped into his body sending him spinning over the desk and crashing into the door through which he had just entered. He was dead before he hit the floor.

The killer holstered his .44, turned and hurried out of the back of the jailhouse. He was on his horse and was galloping away before anybody came running to see what had happened to Sheriff Dolan.

The gunman rode hard into the darkness, satisfied that another threat had been snuffed out.

Mollie Cooper was sleeping deeply, her even breathing the only sound breaking the stillness of the night. Beside her, Ben McCabe stared up at the ceiling, his thoughts far away from the bliss of an hour earlier. Carefully, he slipped out of the bed, pulled on his pants and crept silently across the room, down the stairs and out on to the veranda. It was a starlit night with only a gentle breeze and occasional high cloud.

But McCabe was not there to admire the beauty of the night. He rolled himself a cigarette and leaned on the veranda rail, peering out at the few steers visible in the moonlight.

Somewhere out there was the killer of Dave Dexter and unless he found him and cleared Tommy Kane's name this budding romance with Mollie would be over almost before it started. It would not be too long before the law came calling at the Cooper spread and the last thing he needed was to have Mollie involved. He stared at the red glow of his cigarette and came to a decision. Tomorrow he would show his hand.

The evidence that had convicted Tommy of Dave Dexter's killing had come from four witnesses. A fifth, Buck Dexter, never claimed to have seen the shooting, but the jury had taken the word of the others – Alec Dexter, Joe Kelly, Zeb Maddox and Moose – to reach their verdict.

Yet somebody – maybe all of them – had lied and Ben would find out who that was. He was convinced one of those four had killed Dave. But who? And why?

He was about to go back indoors when he spotted the rider silhouetted against the night sky. He was approaching from the west at a slow, almost walking pace. He disappeared briefly behind a cluster of rocks but emerged into the moonlight barely 200 yards from the house. He was making no secret of his approach but Ben stepped back into the shadows of the overhanging roof of the house.

The rider eventually drew his horse to a halt and leaned forward on the horn of his saddle, pushing back the brim of his hat as he did so. It was an action Ben had seen before. He came out of the darkness and greeted the newcomer with a friendly wave.

'Tommy Kane, just when I was thinking about you, here you are.'

115

Tommy dismounted and climbed the steps. The two men hugged and went inside the house.

Mollie stood at the back of the small crowded church. Around her, groups of Rico townswomen all dressed in similar dark clothes stared and whispered behind hands that held lace handkerchiefs. They had never seen the Cooper woman in the church before, so why now? Of course, Jake Dexter had been a neighbour but hardly a close family friend; and since the break-up of her romance with that handsome son Buck they understood there was some bad feeling between them. That was the gossip around town, anyway, and the women of Rico were not the sort of ladies to allow a good item of gossip pass without comment and further investigation. So, instead of listening to the preacher they studied the slender woman in black standing alone at the rear of the congregation.

For her part, Mollie wondered briefly just how many of the sombre-faced women were there as genuine mourners for Jake Dexter.

Occupying the front row, Buck Dexter stood tall and straight, while his stepmother leaned heavily on him for support. By his side was Alec who hardly looked the part of a grieving son, though Mollie knew that the younger of the brothers always acted as though he had the weight of the world on his shoulders. Now, with his right arm in a sling, he cast a forlorn figure.

Vaguely, the words of the clergyman, the Reverend Matthew Watkins, penetrated her thoughts.

'. . . it would be foolish, my friends, to pretend that Jacob Dexter was universally loved. No man, not even the

Good Lord Himself, who taught us nothing but love, could claim such. But here we are today, in this crowded church, to pay our respects to a man who built our town – built this very church – and who will be missed by so many people from cattlemen to the small farmers and through the town's businessmen whom he gave his support and . . .'

The eulogy continued with Reverend Watkins's voice reaching ever higher levels of praise for the man in the casket until, eventually, Mollie's attention returned when he said, 'And while we are at prayer we must not forget another of our community who is no longer with us. Sadly, last night, as he returned to carry out his duties, our town sheriff was shot to death in his own office and now lies in the funeral parlour.

'We pray that the perpetrator of this heinous act, the intruder who robbed us of an honest and loyal lawman will be brought to justice.'

Frank Dolan dead! Shot in his own office. As the congregation rose to give full voice to the tune of 'Rock of Ages', Mollie's mind was in a whirl. An unknown intruder had entered the sheriff's office and gunned down Dolan. And on the same night a man whom Dolan had arrested for the murder of Dave Dexter had arrived at her ranch to meet Ben McCabe. She had watched from the bedroom window as the two men embraced and entered her house. Had she imagined it, or was that hug of friendship a sign of some secret triumph? McCabe and Tommy Kane, a convicted killer on the run were now in her home. And for the first time, Mollie felt growing fears that the man she thought was the answer to her maiden's prayer could, after

117

all, be nothing more than a cold-blooded killer.

She left the church and waited in the adjacent grave-yard. Gradually the mourners filed out, led by the reverend and the Dexter family who made their way to the already prepared last resting place of Jacob Dexter.

Maybe this was not the right time, but Mollie did not know where to turn except to the man she had once expected to marry and, as she waited for the procession of mourners to move towards the graveside, she made her decision.

Edging as discreetly as possible towards the Dexters she offered her condolences. Then, keeping her voice barely above a whisper for fear of Elizabeth or Alec overhearing, she said, 'We have to talk, Buck. It's about the killing of Frank Dolan.'

Nodding, Buck guided his sobbing stepmother to the graveside while Alec stared straight ahead – as though the occasion of his father's funeral had nothing to do with him.

TWELVE

Tommy Kane threw up his hands in a gesture of frustration. He sat opposite McCabe on the porch of Mollie Cooper's house and for almost an hour he had tried to find an answer to his friend's questions about the night Dave Dexter died. They had used the time that Mollie was away attending the funeral of Jake Dexter to recap the events in the White Horse, and a few fateful minutes later, in the alley behind the hat shop that had been the scene of Dave's murder.

Tommy slapped his lap and got to his feet and clasped his fists in exasperation.

'All I know is that Dave had something to tell me, something he couldn't say to his father or his brothers. If only I knew what it was, maybe. . . .'

McCabe put his arm around the young man's shoulder.

'Whatever it was, Tommy, I think we can reckon it's what got him killed. Anything else is too much of a coincidence and I'm not one for believing in coincidences when somebody ends up with a bullet in his back.'

Ben leaned on the porch rail and studied the open

range. He thought about Mollie at the funeral of Jake Dexter, how she had persuaded herself that she should be there because the Dexters were neighbours and it was expected. He even felt a pang of unreasonable jealousy that Buck would be there and it was unavoidable that they would speak.

Suddenly he spun round. 'Like you say, whatever it was Dave had to tell you – it was something he could not tell his own father or his brothers. Or' – he paused before adding slowly – 'something he had already told them and they had done nothing. What has been going on at the DX?'

Tommy shrugged, a gesture of helplessness. 'I don't know unless it had something to do with the rustling.'

McCabe did not try to hide his surprise. 'The DX has been losing beef?'

Tommy nodded. 'Seems it's been going on for a couple of months, just a few head at first, then a few more.'

'And Jake Dexter and his sons didn't know?'

'I don't know about the old man, but I'm sure the sons knew but, well, I dunno really, it was just something about the place. Joe Kelly posted men on the fences, but the rustlers seemed to know exactly where they were and raided somewhere else.'

Ben felt a sudden surge of optimism. 'That's got to be it, Tommy. Dave was killed for what he knew, for what he was going to tell you.'

'But why didn't he go straight to the sheriff?'

Ben waved away the protest.

'Because he didn't trust Dolan. If he'd gone to him what would the sheriff have done?'

Tommy shrugged.

'Nothing!' Ben snapped. 'Don't you see? If he told Dolan what he knew the sheriff would have gone straight to the man who owned him – Jake Dexter. If Dave had wanted Jake to know what he had found out he would have told him – he wouldn't have come looking for you. Whatever it was Dave had found out he wanted to keep it from his father. By telling you he would leave his best friend to do the right thing.'

Tommy thought for a moment and then, as though a light had been shone in his face, he said, 'So, what you're saying is that Dave didn't go to Jake because. . . .' His voice tailed off.

'He would be betraying somebody at the DX. Somebody Jake trusted so much that he wouldn't be believed.'

'But that's crazy.'

'Is it? Unless I'm mistaken, Dave knew something about the DX that had to be kept secret. And it cost him his life. How would the old man react if he knew that he was being robbed by his own foreman, or even worse, his own son?'

Tommy's mind was racing. Could it be possible? Could Alec Dexter, or Joe Kelly be the men at the head of the gang of rustlers? Tommy had never liked Kelly and could believe anything about him, but Alec – sure he was a hothead and always felt he was being treated badly because Buck was his father's favourite son.

But if what Ben was saying was true it would mean Alec had shot down his own half-brother in cold blood. Even Alec wasn't that evil.

Eventually, it was Ben who spoke.

121

'Tommy, you've got to tell me everything about the night Dave was killed. If I'm right, then one of those who said they saw you shoot Dave is the real killer.'

Tommy Kane didn't care for the White Horse saloon with its smoke-filled rooms of gamblers and girls of loose morals. He knew his mother wouldn't approve of him drinking in what she would have called 'a den of iniquity' – she always had a way with words – but Dave had sounded very serious when he arranged the meeting.

Clearly he had been worse for drink when he picked a quarrel in the street that afternoon, but he suddenly sobered when Joe Kelly moved in to drag him away.

'Meet me tonight in the saloon. It's important, Tommy. You're my best friend and I've got to tell somebody. You'll know what to do.'

'Tell me now.'

But he hadn't told him and so Tommy had made his way to the White Horse where he stood at the bar, toying with his untouched beer and waiting for his friend to arrive.

He tried to avoid eye contact with any of the customers, especially that DX ranch hand with the twisted smile that rarely left his face: Munroe. He was close by engrossed in a card game which appeared to be going badly.

The barman looked Tommy over suspiciously. He couldn't remember having seen the kid in the saloon before and he looked as though he was waiting for somebody. He checked that the pistol he kept under the bar in case of trouble was handy.

Suddenly the batwings burst open and Dave Dexter rushed into the room. Breathless, he immediately spotted Tommy and dashed towards the bar.

Tommy gripped his friends shoulders.

'Hey, slow down. What's the big hurry?'

Gasping for breath, Dave looked frantically around the room. Then, without warning, he pushed Tommy away, sending him back against the bar and knocking over the beer glass.

Tommy made a grab for his friend, but Dave shook himself free, shouting, 'Stay away from me, Tommy. If you know what's good for you. Just stay away.'

With those words he dashed out into the night. Stunned for a moment, Tommy Kane was rooted to the spot. Then, gathering his senses, he apologized to the barman for the spilled drink and ran after his friend.

Main Street was in darkness but Tommy was just able to make out a running figure on the boardwalk outside the ladies' emporium. He was sure it was Dave and he headed off in pursuit.

He yelled after him, 'Dave! Stop!'

But the figure ran on, past the sheriff's office and then in front of the general store. Reaching the hat shop, the running man stopped and then, as if spotting somebody he did not want to see, cut into the alley leading to the stable yard. Tommy followed.

He was only a few feet away when the shots were fired. Two of them – followed by screams of pain.

'Dave!'

Close by, the victim of the shots slumped out of the shadows and fell at Tommy's feet. Then, as he lifted his friend's head, he heard another sound, a thud in the dust at his side. Without thinking, he picked up the gun and was holding it when his friend breathed his last words.

'Tommy . . . Alec – I'm sorry.' Dave Dexter died in his friend's arms.

Spinning round, Tommy Kane saw two figures racing towards

him. In panic, he turned and sprinted for the bottom of the alley.
But he never made it.

Before he could reach the cover and security of the total darkness, he was sent spinning to the ground by a hefty shoulder charge that knocked the breath out of him just as another gunshot shattered the silence and the bullet smashed into the wooden fencing of the stable yard.

'Hold it! I've got him!' The man who had slammed into Tommy stood over him. It was a voice he recognized immediately: Buck Dexter.

Ben McCabe had listened to Tommy's story and had only one question to ask when his friend had finished reliving the night of the killing. 'You're sure that was what Dave said? "Tommy. Alec. I'm sorry".'

'Those were his words as I remember, Ben. I don't know what he was sorry for but he meant the words for me and his brother.'

McCabe didn't answer that. It wasn't what he was thinking. Dave Dexter had gone out of his way to pass on something to his friend, but had been frightened off in the bar of the White Horse. It had been important enough to get him killed. And the only other name on his lips the night he died was his half-brother Alec and from what Tommy had told him the pair were not exactly the best of friends. So, there must have been some other reason for Dave to use his half-brother's name the second he died.

Ben now believed he knew who had the answer to why Dave Dexter was killed and just as vitally, why Tommy Kane had been found guilty of the murder.

THIRTEEN

Mollie drove her buggy away from the funeral of Jake Dexter, taking the long route back to the Cooper ranch. It gave her time to reflect on what a fool she had been. She had been taken in by the handsome stranger with two names and the fresh-faced kid who had been convicted of Dave Dexter's murder, but had been broken out of jail and had convinced her of his innocence.

But now she could see it had been lies. All lies. The evidence had been overwhelming. In addition to the witnesses, he had been trapped by Buck Dexter trying to flee from the scene of the murder. And he had left behind the gun that had killed Dave. Kane's own gun. Why had she allowed herself to be swayed by the man who had so recently come into her life?

The very night that Kane reappeared at the ranch, Sheriff Frank Dolan had been gunned down in his own office by an intruder. And who, more than the Kane kid, could want Dolan dead?

Mollie had no fondness for the lecherous sheriff, but his murder was surely no matter of chance and she knew she had to tell somebody of her suspicions. And the fact that the man she felt responsible was at her house.

Who better to tell of her fears than Buck?

The mourners were drifting away when Mollie eventually managed to get Buck to one side and tell him what she suspected. He listened to what she had to say without interrupting and when she had finished, he took her arm and led her out of earshot of any chance eavesdropper.

'Don't worry, Mollie. I'll handle this, but what I want you to do is stay away from the house for a couple of hours.'

Now, as she stood in the shade of one of the trees over-hanging the creek, she began to wonder about his advice 'to go somewhere you can relax for a few hours and put this out of your head. By tonight the whole thing will be over.'

So she had done as he suggested – but why had she chosen this place? Despite the heat of the early afternoon sun, she felt a sudden shiver. Had she set up Ben McCabe and the kid for a shoot-out? And, if she had, did it matter? The kid had killed Dave Dexter and probably Frank Dolan as well. McCabe had helped him to escape from jail – he had admitted as much – so they were guilty together. And she had lied to Buck about selling the Cooper spread, which meant she owed him something.

But she could not shake off the one niggling doubt in her mind: if Tommy Kane was guilty of two murders why had he come back? Why was he not heading for Mexico or California?

And why was Ben McCabe still around?

Although her conscience troubled her, she tried to convince herself that Buck would offer them the chance to give themselves up. He would not be party to a lynching. But what about the others? Kelly and the Canadian they called Moose – she was not sure about them. And then there was that mean-spirited gambler who had joined the DX crew only a few weeks ago. He was trouble.

And suppose she was wrong? Suppose the kid was innocent – or at the very least McCabe believed him to be innocent? What then?

As she stared into the cool waters of the creek sparkling in the sun, Mollie Cooper realized she could have stirred up a hornets' nest. And it was too late to do anything about it. The late afternoon sun was still hot, but Mollie guessed that Buck had had his couple of hours. It was time to head home.

It was Tommy who spotted them first. There were seven, maybe eight, riders and they were in a hurry and they were not on their way to pay a neighbourly call.

McCabe had already become concerned that Mollie was still not back from the funeral long after she had promised to be home.

He followed the direction of Tommy's pointing finger. The riders were less than a mile away.

'Eight of them,' he guessed aloud 'and we don't know eight people who like us enough to pay a friendly visit, Tommy. It's time to move out.' Racing inside the house the pair grabbed their gunbelts and dashed out to the corral. There was no way of avoiding the fact that they would be seen, their horses were tethered out front in the direct eyeline of the approaching riders.

With an eye on the fast approaching dust cloud, McCabe and Tommy saddled their horses and were on the trail at full gallop and heading south in double quick time.

'Who are they, Ben? And how did they know we were here?'

McCabe didn't answer. Instead, he said, 'Just get your head down, Tommy and get outa here. Remember, their horses will already be tired. If these two have any legs they'll not catch us before nightfall.' His thoughts were racing almost as fast as the steed under him as the fugitives put distance betwen themselves and their pursuers. There was only one answer to Tommy's question. Mollie must have told them. But why?

Her failure to return from the funeral of Jake Dexter could have meant only one thing – she had been told to stay away from the house by whoever was leading the posse of chasers. And it was more than a wild guess that led McCabe to think that the man at the head of the fast-approaching riders was Buck Dexter. Although he found it hard to believe that Mollie would deliberately give them away, what other explanation could there be?

Tommy Kane, the kid they all believed had killed Dave, was out of the territory and heading for Wyoming. Unless somebody had told them differently – and Mollie was the only one who could have betrayed them. There could be only one reason: something had happened to convince her to turn them in. But what? McCabe was baffled.

'They're gaining on us!'

There was fear in Tommy's gasping voice, but McCabe ignored him. The chasers were losing ground, just as he had expected, their horses were tiring.

Over to the right the forest of pines offered the chance of cover but with at least eight riders hot on their tails, they could fan out and surround them. It would be only a matter of time before they closed in. To the left the open plain offered no hiding place.

Straight ahead was the gorge where, if luck was with them, they could find a refuge and double back when the chance came.

The chase was on, but another mile of hard riding took Ben and Tommy deep into the canyon and out of sight of their pursuers. And there to their right was a gap in the rockery that offered a bolt hole to hide. Buck and his men were out of sight and Ben knew that they might not get a better chance to shake them off.

The gap between boulders was just wide enough to squeeze their horses through and once the other side they were able to take up a hidden position, but still able to keep a close watch on Dexter's men.

Dismounting and leading their horses out of sight, they crouched behind the rocks, rifles and six-guns at the ready. If it came to a shoot-out, the odds were stacked four-to-one against them and they needed every advantage they could get.

They had hardly settled when the sound of pounding hoofs signalled the arrival of the posse.

Crouching as low as they could without losing sight of the oncoming riders, McCabe and the kid tensed themselves for the worst. But as they approached at full gallop with Buck and his foreman Joe Kelly at the head they showed no signs of slowing and it was all the pair could do to keep their relief in check.

129

But the joy of seeing their pursuers ride off on their fruitless chase lasted no more than a second for Ben McCabe. The sight of the third man in the group changed everything: Jay Munroe.

As the eight riders disappeared in a cloud of dust around a distant bend, McCabe rose to his feet. They mounted up and headed back the way they had come. Ben was grim-faced and silent until they reached the mouth of the canyon where he suddenly reined in his horse.

Surprised, Tommy pulled up alongside him. 'What's wrong? Why're we stopping?'

Ben leaned forward. He spoke slowly but there was authority in his voice. 'Tommy, I want you to keep on riding and don't stop until you reach that hotel where you left that pretty girl of yours. Then I want you to take her off to your place in Wyoming and marry her. Now, get going before they find we've doubled back and come after us.'

Tommy opened his mouth to protest, but McCabe waved him away. He knew it was only a matter of time before he came face to face with Jay Munroe and this was now personal. He didn't want Tommy Kane around when killing time came.

'This isn't your fight any more. There's going to be some shooting and Ellie and your mother don't need a message to say that you're just another unmarked cross in Boot Hill.'

'But, Ben, I can't leave you—'

McCabe knew that his reasoning wasn't working. Tommy was a good kid – he had come back when he could have been hundreds of miles away – so he tried the angry approach. 'Look, I can't watch your back as well as my own. Munroe's a real snake. He gunned down my old railroad boss and then he knifed a saloon girl. He's a mean killer and now he knows I'm around he'll come running and I want to be waiting.

'*You would only get in my way.*'

The emphasis in McCabe's tone stunned Tommy, but before he could say anything, the other repeated his order. 'Now get going.'

Without another word, Tomy swung his horse away and headed for the open plains that would eventually lead him out of the territory. McCabe sat and watched him go and there was more relief than sadness when he eventually disappeared from view. He knew that if he didn't find the real killer of Dave Dexter and settle with Jay Munroe the pair of them would be living in the shadow of the noose. McCabe turned his horse in the direction of the Cooper ranch and his confrontation with Mollie.

FOURTEEN

The horse tied to the rail at the foot of the steps had been ridden hard and was heavily lathered in sweat. Mollie paused before alighting from her buggy. She knew the horse and she had not expected to see it again – not after what she had told Buck Dexter.

But Ben McCabe was waiting for her and although there was no sign of anger in his face she already knew him well enough to realize that he was not a man given to indignation or rage.

'Why did you do it, Mollie?' he asked, without the politeness of any preliminaries. 'Why did you send Buck Dexter and his crew after us?'

'You know why, Ben,' she said, throwing her funeral hat on to a chair.

'Tell me. You see, I really thought you believed in me and Tommy, I thought—'

'So did I, Ben, until last night,' she interrupted angrily. 'Until Tommy Kane killed Frank Dolan!'

'Dolan's dead?' Mollie looked closely at the McCabe's expression. Was the surprise genuine? Did he really not know? Then his expression changed.

'And you think Tommy killed him?'

She said nothing.

McCabe slumped into an armchair. He felt deflated and angry. And hurt because the woman who had just come into his life had betrayed him. But worse than that – he knew she was wrong.

'Tommy Kane hasn't killed anybody,' he said at last. 'Why can't you believe that?'

'He was found guilty of murdering Dave Dexter,' she said, but there was a lack of conviction in her voice. 'Then he goes on the run and the night he turns up here the sheriff is shot down in his own office.'

'Why would Tommy come back here to kill Frank Dolan?' McCabe protested. 'He was on his way to Wyoming to marry his sweetheart, Ellie Jacobs.'

'But he did come back!' Mollie shouted. 'And now Frank Dolan is dead. He was the one who arrested the Kane boy. I don't know – maybe he just wanted some sort of vengeance – an eye for an eye.'

'Sit down, Mollie,' McCabe said quietly, when she had finished. 'The least you can do is hear me out while I still have the time. It won't take Buck Dexter long to know where we shook him off. He'll be back soon and heading this way. I want to be out of here before he and his gunmen come in looking for blood.'

Mollie took the chair he had vacated and sat with her hands in her lap. She looked nervous, tense.

'Tommy didn't come back here to kill Dolan; he came back because he thought he was deserting me, leaving me to sort out his troubles.

'I want you to listen to me, Mollie, because what I'm going to say is the nearest you'll get to the truth until I can give you the proof we need.' Mollie said nothing.

'The night Dave was killed he had arranged to meet Tommy. He had said it was important so when he arrived at the White Horse Tommy was waiting for him. But before Dave could say anything he suddenly turned on Tommy, who thinks his friend saw somebody who scared the hell out of him. He shouted at Tommy to leave him alone and dashed out of the bar. Tommy went after him and caught up with him in the alley behind the hat shop. He called after him and then he heard two shots and saw Dave fall. He was kneeling over him when somebody threw a gun into the alley. Tommy picked it up. It was his own Colt that he had left back at the DX when he left. He was kneeling over Dave when Buck spotted him. Tommy ran off, but Buck caught him at the end of the alley.'

He paused before adding, 'But Dave wasn't quite dead, and before he died his last word to Tommy was: "Alec".'

'Alec? And what do you think he meant?'

'I don't know, but there's something going on at the DX that they don't want known around these parts. And unless I'm guessing wrong, Alec's involved. And it's what got Dave Dexter killed. That I'm pretty sure of.'

Mollie got to her feet. 'And what else are you sure of? Maybe that it was Alec who shot Dave and threw that gun so that your friend would pick it up? That Alec killed his own brother? Are you crazy?'

McCabe chuckled but there was no humour in the sound. 'He wouldn't be the first, Mollie.'

He picked up his hat from the table and made to leave.

'I know Tommy didn't kill Dave Dexter and, yeah, maybe it was Alec who pulled the trigger. But whatever's been happening up at the DX Alec is sure to be part of it. And any outfit that hires a killer like Jay Munroe can't be on the side of the good guys.'

The name meant nothing to Mollie and Ben made no attempt to explain. Instead, he put on his hat and headed for the door. He turned towards her and said with a hint of sadness, 'I'm real sorry it didn't work for us, Mollie. I really thought we might have something going. Seems not.

'And as for you thinking that Alec killing his brother is crazy, wasn't it a coupla brothers who started all this murdering in the first place? Or ain't you ever heard of Cain and Abel?'

He left her standing watching his back as he mounted his already tired horse and led it slowly away from the house for the last time.

Alec Dexter eased himself slowly down from the buggy and made his way into the house. Although the pain from his wound had abated, he was in no fit state to follow Buck and the others on their manhunt. With one arm in a sling he had a ready-made reason to back out.

Not that the idea would have entered his head even if he had been fit and able to ride at full speed. He had no intention of putting himself at risk to chase halfway across the territory after the Kane kid and his sidekick, McCabe.

That was Buck's job. Now that the old man was in the ground, the ranch would pass on to his brother. It was up to him and Kelly and the rest of them to hunt down killers. Alec had far more important matters to deal with.

But first things first – his stepmother needed a ride home from the funeral and although Alec had never warmed to his father's second wife, he took the opportunity to volunteer to ride the buggy to the ranch.

The homeward journey was made in a series of long silences broken only by the widow's occasional bursts of sobbing. Alec had delivered her to the house and now she would soon be inside, alone with her tears. Alec had no time for that. The old man was dead and buried. This was the time for the living and he had things to do.

Now that Dolan was dead there was one less to share the spoils from the cattle rustling and the stage hold-ups by the renegades. But the Indians were getting greedy. The next whiskey and few rounds of ammunition would be the last. Alec Dexter was getting out. California, maybe. Or Texas. That was a big open country so he'd heard. And there'd be no old man or Buck to give him orders.

Alec had helped the grieving widow up the steps and into the house. He wondered briefly how she would cope without a husband and with her own son hardly cold in the ground. But the thought soon passed. He had his own life ahead of him and that would start as soon as he was clear of the ranch.

'You going to be all right?' he asked, without enthusiasm.

'I'll be fine,' Elizabeth said quietly. 'I'll go up to my room. If you could just tell Martha I won't be down for dinner tonight, but she's to cook for you and Buck as usual.'

Alec nodded. He could survive without old Martha's cooking, but, as he had no plans to be around come sup-

136

pertime he hardly felt it was worth passing on the message.

'I'll see to it,' he said. 'You get some rest.'

He watched his stepmother slowly climb the wide staircase and waited for her to move along the corridor to her room before going to his father's desk and withdrawing the key of the safe.

As swiftly as he could under the handicap of his injuries he made his way across the room. Then, fumbling in his haste to open the safe – as though he expected to be interrupted at any moment – he heaved a sigh of relief when the door eventually opened smoothly.

Casting aside the piles of official papers that no doubt included his father's will and other files on the DX ranch, he reached deep into the rear of the safe and it was all he could do to restrain himself from a shout of triumph as his fingers folded around one neatly wrapped bundle of notes. Then another.

Throwing back the papers that were of no interest to him, Alec slammed the door closed, stuffed the cash into his bag and then returned the key to his father's desk drawer.

He figured that the $10-$15,000 in his bag was a small price for them to pay for shutting him out of their lives all these years. Buck was the worst: always ordering him around the place while the old man doted all his affection on his youngest, Dave.

Well now Davey-boy was gone as well as his father; and now it was Alec's turn to get out – though he wasn't going in a wooden box. No, sir. This money from the safe, plus the cash he'd stored in the deserted mine shaft from the stage robberies by the renegades would be enough to set him up in California. Or Texas. They'd all thought he was a fool. Well, who was the fool now? Buck would be left to work his butt off while he enjoyed a life of women and saloons.

Alec shook himself out of his reverie and left the house and went to the back of the barn where he had left his own buckboard ready loaded. He threw the newly filled carpetbag into the back and climbed aboard.

'Planning to go somewhere, Dexter?'

Alec spun round. He had not spotted the figure leaning against the side of the barn. He had expected the ranch to be deserted. All the hands were either at the funeral, or had joined Buck and Kelly chasing after McCabe and the kid. All except the man now eyeing him with that sick smirk on his face: Jay Munroe.

'What you doin' here, Jay? I thought you'd be chasing after that old friend of yours, McCabe. Maybe you'd get him for real this time.' He tried to make the suggestion sound like a lighthearted jibe but Munroe wasn't taken in.

'Your brother couldn't find his own ass in a bathtub. He led us up that canyon while McCabe turned tail and went back the way we'd come. Now he's leading them all over the South-west. I decided to leave them chasing their own shadows and come back here to see my old friend Alec. Now I find he's all loaded up and ready to leave without paying out what he owes. Looks like you can't be trusted.'

Alec tried to hide the anxiety with a grin.

'Guess it does look that way, but you know better, Jay. Hey, who brought you into this outfit? Why would I run out on you now?'

Munroe threw down a half-smoked cheroot, pushed

himself away from the barn wall and took the reins of the buckboard horse.

'Let's just think about that, Alec. Dolan's dead, your old man's buried and McCabe and the kid are on the loose. And, unless I'm wrong, McCabe knows that Kane didn't kill Dave.' He paused. 'Seems to me things are getting pretty sticky for you around here and could be the right time to be moving on.'

'Look, Jay, you've got this wrong. I ain't running out. I've got to keep those renegades sweet if we want them to carry on with those stage and rail jobs. That's what's in this buckboard. Whiskey and guns, that's what makes them happy.'

Munroe nodded. 'I've already had a look-see so I know what's in there. I reckon we should go to your meeting together. That way I can be sure.' Alec could see no way out and when Munroe hitched his horse to the back of the buckboard and jumped up alongside him he knew he would have to think fast when the time came to act. Right now it was time to go along with Munroe and let him think that what he had been told was the truth.

McCabe was dismounting to give his horse another much needed rest when he spotted the buckboard with the two men up front and the saddled horse trotting along at the back. Dusk was falling and at first sight it was nothing more that a couple of workers going about their normal business and, with his thoughts elsewhere, he paid little attention to the scene below.

Mollie was now in the past; Tommy Kane was on his way back to the family farm with a new bride-to-be and he, Ben

McCabe, was again a man alone. A man unsure of his own future, but certain that Mollie Cooper would not be involved. She had betrayed him and even though he believed that her intentions were good, Ben could not see beyond the fact that she had turned against Tommy and himself. It was all a matter of trust. She had believed that Tommy had killed the Rico sheriff and, without even a word to Ben, she had gone straight to her former lover Buck Dexter.

McCabe's thought turned to Tommy's mother, Elspeth Kane, the woman who had once helped to save his life and whose plea for help he had answered when he rode into Rico in an attempt to clear the boy's name. He had failed in that quest, but Tommy was free and was heading for home. He could almost see Elspeth's face as she welcomed her elder son back into the house.

That left only Jay Munroe and McCabe's thirst for vengeance was growing. Munroe's two bullets had failed to kill him but they had changed his life.

Rubbing down his horse, McCabe let his gaze wander to the valley below. The buckboard was getting closer and the two men appeared to be involved in a heated quarrel. But it wasn't his concern.

He had decided that it was time to head for Rico. Now that Frank Dolan was dead there was only the young deputy to recognise him, or connect him with the jail-break, and he felt it was worth the risk to start there if he was ever to find the killer of Dave Dexter.

But his plans were abruptly interrupted when a group of riders suddenly emerged from a cluster of trees on the far side of the valley and headed towards the buckboard.

At first, Ben paid little attention until he realized that the horsemen were not a group of passing cowboys but six or seven Indians.

He had heard stories of renegades on the loose in the district and there had been witnesses' tales that they were connected with a series of stage robberies.

Intrigued, McCabe dropped to his haunches and studied the scene below. Were the two men on the buckboard about to come under attack? They were too far out of range for McCabe to be of any help. All he could do was sit and watch.

But what happened next stirred his curiosity. One of the Indians dismounted and walked around the back of the buckboard and jumped aboard. Then he signalled to one of his colleagues who approached the buckboard. Others joined him and as McCabe studied the scene he quickly realized what was happening.

He was watching two men trading with the Indians.

Two of the Indians dragged a long box off the back of the wagon and the two men climbed down – one of them walking with a slight limp and appeared to have his arm in a sling – and the leader of the Indians tossed down a bundle which the limping man tried to catch one-handed but it fell to the ground. There was a lot of shouting and arm-waving among the renegades who eventually, satisfied with the trade, spun their horses and headed off in the direction they had come.

The buckboard driver picked up the bundle and the two men studied the contents before climbing aboard.

McCabe waited for the two men to restart their journey before mounting up. Who were they? And was the scene he had just witnessed connected to the killing of Dave Dexter? And maybe Rico's sheriff? And where were they heading? McCabe knew the only way he could discover the answers to these questions was the follow them.

The trail through the valley veered off to the west and McCabe had a lot of ground to make up if he was to keep them in his sights.

He knew his horse was not refreshed enough to endure another long hard ride. But luck was on his side. The men were in no hurry to reach their destination and, after guiding his horse down the tricky slopes through the bushes and on to the plain below, the buckboard was still in clear view.

McCabe knew that he could not risk getting too close but without taking a chance he might never discover the identity of the men.

It was a slow pursuit, punctuated by the need to steer his horse through the sparodic cover of the bushland out of sight of the duo. He was beginning to wonder if the two men had any specific plans when they suddenly turned off the trail and forced him to turn back into the bushes for fear of discovery. He crouched down to watch the pair up ahead.

They manouevred the wagon and the horse tied at the back into the shade of the trees and made their way towards a small shack at the head of an old abandoned copper mine.

They disappeared into the ramshackle building and it was several minutes before they came back into McCabe's view. Ben cursed his lack of a spy glass as he tried to follow the movements of the pair.

One of them threw a carpetbag into the wagon while the other went to untie his horse. The pair were going their separate ways.

McCabe watched and waited. The two men exchanged words – although he could not hear what was said the gestures indicated that the pair were not parting on the best of terms – and there was anger in the way the taller man pulled his horse loose from the buckboard and mounted up. Then, digging his heels viciously into the animal's sides he set off at a gallop. And he was heading straight for the spot where McCabe was hiding.

Crouching, McCabe unholstered his Colt in readiness. He needed no telling that anybody who had been trading with renegade Indians would be the kind of man to shoot first and ask questions later.

But, as the rider got ever closer, all ideas of trading with Indians or any other kind of illegal activity were banished from his thoughts. There was no mistaking the man coming his way, dressed in black, with long lank hair, thin features and an untidy moustache. It had been a long time but it was a face McCabe could never forget. Only a few yards away was the man who had left him for dead in a Wyoming creek. Ben McCabe rose to his feet and stared into the eyes of Jay Munroe.

It was all over in a matter of moments. As Ben stepped out from the undergrowth and fired a shot skywards, Munroe's startled horse reared up and threw its rider to the ground.

The horse bolted and McCabe knew he could have gunned down Munroe there and then without another thought. The man was a ruthless killer – he deserved nothing better than a swift bullet. But even that was too good for him – Ben wanted him to know who had stepped out of the bushes, scared his horse and eventually rid the West of one more heartless murderer.

'On your feet, Munroe,' Ben snapped. 'I'm gonna give you a better chance than you ever gave anybody in your whole worthless life.'

Munroe rose slowly to his feet. The twisted grin never left his face but there was fear in his eyes.

'I ain't gonna draw on you, McCabe. You ain't got no cause—'

Ben fired at his feet, the dust splattering his boots. 'I'm not asking you to draw, Jay. I just want you to know that you've got a choice. Right now, I've got about five seconds of waiting time left in me. Once that's gone—' He fired again, this time the bullet ripping through the leather of Munroe's left boot. It was more than the killer could take. He reached for his own Colt, but it had not cleared the holster on his left hip before McCabe fired again – this time straight at the other man's chest. Then, another bullet to the stomach. And a third.

The jerking body of Jay Munroe thrashed briefly in the dust and then lay still.

Ben holstered his own gun, strolled the hundred or so yards to where Munroe's horse had decided to settle and graze, and led the animal back to where the body was lying. Lifting Munroe's remains into the saddle, he tied his wrists to one of the stirrups, his ankles to the other and then collected his own horse.

Munroe may have been a no-good thief and killer, but

144

McCabe was going to give him something he didn't deserve. A decent burial.

Alec Dexter heard the gunshots and instinctively pulled the wagon to a halt. Turning in his seat, he was horrified to see the scene along the valley. Even at a distance and in the fading light, he could make out the figure of a man lying motionless and another, gun in hand, standing over him.

It was as clear as day what had happened. Munroe had got his chance to finish off the man called Ben McCabe and this time he had lost. There could be no doubt that the man standing over the body was McCabe.

Gripping the reins, Alec ignored the pain of his wounds and lashed his horse into action. He cursed his luck. His dead partner lying a few hundred yards away was already banished from his mind, his thoughts turned to his own future.

Buck and the others would still be out looking for McCabe, and here he was within killing range if Alec only had the use of both hands.

Panic suddenly seized him. Maybe his name was on McCabe's list . . . maybe he was out to get them all for putting the Kane kid behind bars. Maybe. . . .

How long would it take a gunslinger like McCabe to track him down? Alone, out there in the wilds, there would be no place for him to hide.

Alec knew he had only one chance – to get back to the DX where he could feel safe in the knowledge that even a man like McCabe would not be crazy enough to tangle with a whole crowd of ranch hands.

With luck on his side Alec could return the money to the safe before anybody knew it was missing. Then, once the threat from McCabe was over – once Buck or one of the others had rid them of the meddling drifter – he could return to his original plan now that Munroe was dead. Urging on his horse, Alec Dexter checked that he was not being followed but it was only when the DX house came into view that he felt he could relax. There was no sign of any of the ranch hands or their horses. The place was deserted except, he assumed, for his stepmother who would still be in her room shedding her tears.

Once inside the house, Alec returned the stolen cash to the safe then, searching through a drinks cupboard he withdrew a bottle of whiskey and a glass and threw himself into an armchair. He felt a sudden surge of daring, almost wishing McCabe to come to the house.

He gulped the first glass of the whiskey and, pouring another, thought about what he had seen: Jay Munroe lying in the dust with the killer standing over him.

The shooting of Munroe was a damned annoyance and expensive. He had already taken his share of the loot which meant either that McCabe had helped himself, or the money was rotting in a dead man's saddle-bag.

Alec poured himself a third drink and cursed his luck.

Where the hell were Buck and the others? By the time Alec Dexter dropped off into a heavy sleep the whiskey bottle was almost empty. . . .

FIFTEEN

Curiosity caused the residents of Rico to stand and stare as the tall stranger in the saddle led the horse and its lifeless bundle down the main street before pulling up outside the undertaker's. The women pointed and whispered and the men looked on with mild interest.

It was early morning but already the workers of Rico were going about their business.

McCabe dismounted beside the funeral parlour sign and was greeted by a small, fussy man who came out of the undertaker's wiping his hands on a towel.

It had been a busy few days for Aristotle Beam. First, Jake Dexter had been given the sort of send-off never before seen in Rico; then Sheriff Frank Dolan was buried without much ceremony the previous morning; now another customer was being delivered to his door. Aristotle was not given to regular bouts of smiling but trade was brisk and it was the nature of his business to thrive on the grief and misfortunes of others. 'Death for some is life for others,' he was fond of saying.

McCabe wrapped the reins of the horses around the rail.

'The name's Jay Munroe,' he said, without the preamble of introductions.

A look of surprise crossed Aristotle Beam's round face. 'From the DX? Alec Dexter's friend?'

'Reckon so,' McCabe said guardedly.

'Who's paying?' Beam asked, examining the dried blood and the bullet holes in the body.

'Check his saddle-bags and I'm sure you'll find enough to cover it and maybe some more. If not, sell the horse.'

He started to walk away towards the sheriff's office, but Beam called him back.

'Did you kill him, mister?'

When McCabe said nothing, the little undertaker added, 'If you did, the least thing you can do is help me carry him inside.'

McCabe nodded and went back to offer his help. His next stop was the railroad depot and the telegraph office. Once there he scribbled his message, threw a few dollar bills on to the desk and ordered the telegraph officer to send the message right away. The man read through the few words, noted the name on the top and nodded.

'I'll get it done.'

'Make sure you do, fella, and if anybody asks about it you don't know a thing,' Ben told him.

Then he rode out of town, no longer in any doubt. It was time to call on the man he believed to be the real killer of Dave Dexter.

Alec groaned, his bleary eyes and aching head an instant reminder, if one was needed, of how he spent the hour before falling into a sleep. The discarded whiskey bottle and broken glass lying at his feet offered further evidence of his heavy drinking.

Staggering to his feet, he looked around the room. It was as he vaguely remembered it – neat and tidy except for the spilled drink near his chair.

But where was Buck? He sure as hell wasn't still looking for McCabe. And what about the others – Kelly, Maddox and the rest?

Even through his fuddled brain, he soon came up with the only possible answer. They had abandoned their chase for McCabe and the Kane kid and had spent the whole night whooping it up in some saloon in Rico or another one-horse town down the valley. Now they were all sleeping it off in some whorehouse or two-bit hotel room. Why hadn't he thought of that before and gone into town to join them? he wondered.

God, how his head hurt.

He reached for the nearby water jug but his hand never quite made it.

'Glad I found you at home,' the voice said.

He had not heard the approaching footsteps, but now as he turned to face the visitor he could only gawp at the broad figure who had appeared in the doorway. The man was bigger than he remembered, but he had only had a brief glimpse of him as he stood over the body of Jay Munroe.

'What the hell are you doin' here? And what do you want?'

McCabe smiled. 'I guess you must be Alec,' he said and when he got no reply he went on, 'I've come to take you in – after we've had our little talk.'

'Look, mister—'

'Sit down. You might as well be comfortable. Oh, and my young friend says sorry about your injuries. Nothing personal.'

Alec slumped back into his chair, any bravado brought on by the previous night's drinking already drained away.

'What do you want?' he asked feebly.

'Among other things, to see you tried for murder.'

Alec sat upright, genuine surprise on his face. 'Who am I supposed to have killed?'

MCabe scoffed. 'You know who, and I figured out why. And I can guess the rest.'

'Look, mister, either you're crazy or somebody's been spreading lies about me. I ain't killed anybody.'

'What about young Dave?'

Alec gasped in astonishment. 'Dave? Dave was my brother.'

'Half-brother. And like I said to somebody else – it didn't stop Cain killing Abel.'

It was Alec's turn to scoff. 'Who are you – some kind of Bible-puncher?' He moved to get up, confidence returning. This stranger was just guessing.

'Tommy Kane killed Davie. He was found guilty and he was gonna hang for it until somebody – you – broke him out of jail.' He stared boldly at the man in the doorway but when the stranger didn't flinch the newfound confidence quickly deserted him.

'Sit down,' McCabe barked. 'Like I said we've got things to discuss and after what I saw this afternoon you're in more trouble than you know. Even if you buy some more witnesses over the killing, you won't talk your way out of trading guns to a band of renegades. That's enough to hang you.'

Alec stayed silent. Who was this man and how much had he seen?

'Trading with runaways – that's bad business in these parts. The way I figure it is this: Dave found out what you were up to and he wanted to tell somebody.

'He couldn't go to Dolan with the information because the sheriff was in it up to his neck. He was a Dexter man. So Dave went to the only real friend he had, Tommy Kane, figuring he would know what to do. After all, you were family.'

'You're crazy!' Alec exploded again. 'You think I killed Dave? I tell you, Kane killed him. And all over that Jacobs girl.'

'Like I was saying, Dave didn't know who to tell about you and the Indians so he went to Tommy for help. You knew they were meeting that night and you followed him into the alley. You killed Dave, threw the gun Tommy had left behind at the ranch when your father sent him packing.'

Alec looked drained but refused to buckle.

'But there were witnesses – Maddox, Moose—'

'Dexter men,' McCabe interrupted fiercely, 'bought and paid for. You killed Dave and you were going to let Tommy Kane hang for it. You and your family paid witnesses to lie' – McCabe knew he was shooting in the dark with this but he went on – 'and after what I saw today I know why. Even a town like Rico wouldn't listen to a family who traded guns to a band of renegade Indians.'

But Alec was no longer listening. Instead he was staring

beyond McCabe at the figure who had slipped silently into the room.

McCabe got no further. For the second time since he had trodden foot on the DX ranch a violent blow to the back of his head sent him into oblivion. . . .

Voices, raised in anger, broke into McCabe's returning consciousness as he slowly emerged from the darkness. He was also vaguely aware that he could not move freely; that his hands and feet were tied and he was again strapped into a chair.

Slowly opening his eyes, McCabe could just make out the blurred figures involved in the heated argument. Suddenly one of them spun round and noticed that the prisoner was recovering consciousness.

He walked across, leaned over the man in the chair and smiled.

'Alec's been telling me how you burst in here and accused him of killing young Dave. How you threatened him if he didn't confess. That's no way for a deputy US marshal to behave, is it, McCabe?'

Buck Dexter turned away. He walked over to a table, picked up a badge and threw it into Ben's lap.

'We found this in your roll. Now why would a deputy US marshal want to keep it a secret?'

Ben's head ached from the blow of what he thought must have been a rifle butt and he was having trouble making sense of his predicament.

Why had Buck hit him without warning, and why was he tied to a chair?

Alec burst out, 'I told you, Buck! He's crazy! He reckons

I killed Dave because he knew something and was going to tell Kane that night. Tell him he's crazy, Buck. Tell him I didn't kill Dave.'

Alec was almost hysterical but his brother remained calm as he perched on the side of the desk.

He waited for Ben to speak but when nothing came he said quietly, 'You should have ridden on by, McCabe and let the law take its course.

'The way I figure it is this. The man who broke a convicted killer out of jail is really a deputy US marshal named Ben McCabe who hides his identity in his saddle roll because . . . well, maybe because helping a killer to dodge justice and escape from the law wouldn't look too good for a man wearing a US marshal's badge.'

'Tommy Kane didn't kill your half-brother,' McCabe protested, his senses slowly returning.

'And you reckon it was Alec over there?

'I told you, Buck, the man's crazy!'

'Shut up!' Buck rapped at his younger brother. 'You've caused this family enough trouble, you and your schemes.'

'What d'ya mean?'

Buck ignored Alec. Instead, he walked slowly across the room, picked up another chair and straddled it alongside Ben.

He stared into McCabe's face – his eyes cold, his features grimly set. 'McCabe knows he ain't gonna walk away from this so I reckon he's entitled to know why he's going to be found down some ravine. Or maybe floating face down in some lake.'

There was a short silence before Buck continued almost with a resigned sigh, 'Dave was unlucky – he was just unlucky.'

'Buck? What're you saying?' Alec's voice was little more than a whisper.

'I said shut up! You and your idle crowd of losers. Thinking nobody knew about your rustling and your dealings with that band of renegades.'

Alec gasped. 'You knew?'

'You fool – everybody knew – everybody except Pa. Oh, he would have let you get away with selling off a few cattle and getting into trouble in town. Hell, he could buy off any trouble and he'd taken a few chances outside the law in his own younger days. But selling guns and whiskey to a bunch of savages – that would have killed him off and sent him to his grave even sooner. You call McCabe crazy! What does that make you, Alec? The old man lost two brothers in the Indian Wars and he was badly shot up so if he found out his own son was trading with the redskins it would have broken him.'

He looked across in disgust at his brother who was now cringing in his seat. Then he turned his attention back to McCabe.

'Dave was out riding when he spotted Alec dealing with the Indians. He told me about it and I promised to put a stop to it. There had already been stories of Indians, drunk on whiskey, attacking stages and making off with strong boxes. When that didn't stop Dave went to the law – and if that didn't work he would have to tell Pa. So he told Dolan, but Frank knew he couldn't arrest Alec so he came to me with the story. He wanted me to buy his silence.

'Dave was friends with young Kane and arranged to meet him in the White Horse. There could be only one

154

reason – and that was to tell him what he knew. Dave was scared and when he spotted Alec's buddy Munroe in the bar, he ran out. His timing couldn't have been better. He headed straight for the alley and ... well, the rest you know.'

Ben stiffened.

'Except I got one thing badly wrong: it wasn't Alec who followed him into that alley, it was you. You killed your own brother.'

'Half-brother,' Buck reminded him. 'I couldn't let him destroy everything we've got here. This is Dexter land; Rico's a Dexter town;

the men are Dexter men. The old man was already dying. I just wanted him to die happy and ignorant. I couldn't let Dave tell Tommy Kane – he'd always said he knew a lawman from way back. I suppose that must be you, McCabe. I had to decide for the old man – his youngest son killed by some drunk in a back alley, or the shame of seeing another son hang for robbery and trading with the Indians.' He paused, then added slowly, 'Like I said, Dave was unlucky.'

'And you killed the sheriff?'

'Dolan got greedy. His silence got too expensive so I had to make it permanent. I'd already got rid of Dave, so with young Kane on the loose and bearing a grudge against Dolan, well, like Dave, the sheriff was in the wrong place—'

Those were the last words to leave Buck Dexter's lips.

A blast from a shotgun shattered the silence and Buck crashed from his chair, blood gushing from a headwound. He was dead before he hit the floor.

Alec yelped and McCabe spun round, sending his own chair crashing on to its side.

At the top of the winding staircase, Elizabeth Dexter let the weapon slip from her grasp and clatter down the wooden staircase.

'He killed my son,' she gasped, her voice little more than a croak. 'He killed my David.' Then she slumped to the floor in a dead faint.

It was then that Joe Kelly burst into the room, his six-gun at the ready and pointing at McCabe.

SIXTEEN

There were four of them around the desk in the Rico sheriff's office. Ben McCabe was wearing his deputy US marshal's badge; Joe Kelly sat alongside the young deputy sheriff Danny Lockwood; the fourth member of the group was a tall, square jawed sandy-haired man in his late thirties. He was dressed in the dark—blue uniform of the US Army.

The soldier stood against the wall, a commanding figure who had taken control of the situation ever since his arrival in town that morning.

It was the day after the death of Buck Dexter. Kelly had burst into the room after hearing the gunshot. After hurried explanations, the confused ranch foreman had freed McCabe and it had taken several minutes to rouse Mrs Dexter from her comatose state while all the time Alec had stared vacantly at the body of his dead brother lying at his feet in a pool of blood.

'And you've got Alec Dexter locked up in a cell back there?' the soldier resumed the discussion.

McCabe nodded.

'I think he's about ready to talk, Captain,' he said. 'I'm just glad you got my telegraph message and could get here. I didn't want our young deputy being left all alone to handle this.'

The soldier smiled. 'Things have been pretty quiet up at Fort Dempsey these past few weeks, so the men are looking for some action. Rounding up a few whiskey-sodden renegades is better than sitting around fighting among themselves.'

'I think you'll find they are more than that, Captain. But Alec will tell you all about them. I'm sure he'll be thinking you might go easy on him in return for a bit of help tracking them down.'

The army man smiled again. 'I think me and my men can be trusted to do our own tracking, Mr McCabe. I'm just curious we hadn't heard of these renegades and the stage robberies before.'

'With the sheriff in on it, he wasn't about to send out messages that would bring the army down on his territory.' Ben got to his feet. 'Besides, I think Kelly here might know enough to help you out.'

The soldier turned to young deputy Danny Lockwood who had remained silent throughout the discussion.

'I'll be back later for the prisoner, young fella. I trust I can leave you in charge till I get back.'

He turned to McCabe.

'Well, thanks again, McCabe. I guess you'll be moving on.'

Ben nodded. 'In a day or two; I've still got one or two things to clear up here.'

The soldier left and the young deputy went out back to

check on his prisoner.

'I'm sorry, I figured you all wrong, Kelly. I guessed you were in on the rustling and on keeping the renegades full of whiskey.'

'Naw. I was only there to keep Alec out of trouble. Looks like I didn't do too good at that. Buck had us all fooled, Marshal. I let him talk me into giving evidence at young Kane's trial. I was under orders, but I really thought Tommy had killed his friend over that Jacobs girl. The gun was in his hand. He was kneeling over the body when Buck stepped out of the dark. The evidence added up. And then when the Moose and Maddox told what they had seen, well – like I said, it added up.'

Suddenly the office door opened behind them and Mollie Cooper stepped into the room. Both men got to their feet.

She appeared flustered and breathless. She nodded a silent greeting to Kelly and then turned to face Ben.

'I hoped I'd find you here,' she said. 'I've just come from the Dexter place. Elizabeth is still in a daze over what's happened, but she's talking of selling up and going back East. She wants me to buy her out.'

Ben waited for her to continue. He could see she was having problems and he was in no mood to help her. He could never forgive her for the way she sold out Tommy to Buck – even if she thought she was doing what was right.

He could understand Elizabeth's desire to get well away from Rico. Her husband had died, her son gunned down in a back alley and she had killed her own stepson because he was the murderer. On top of that her other stepson was behind bars and faced the threat of an army noose for trading with Indians.

The Dexter family was truly cursed.

With these thoughts running through his head, McCabe almost missed Mollie's question.

'Adding the DX to my place will make it too big for me. Will you stick around and help me run the place?'

Ben smiled. 'You got the wrong man, Mollie. I'm no cowhand. The only beef I'm interested in comes on a plate. Now, Joe Kelly here, he could be the man you're looking for.'

Mollie looked unconvinced. She had never liked Kelly, but that didn't mean he wasn't a good foreman.

'Look, Ben, I'm truly sorry about what I did. I really thought—'

McCabe lifted his hat from the back of the chair.

'Like I said, my only interest in beef is how it's cooked. I'll leave you folks to talk things over. Right now, I've got other things to do – like take a trip to Wyoming. I might be in time to attend a friend's wedding.'